RETURN TO
VENGEANCE CREEK

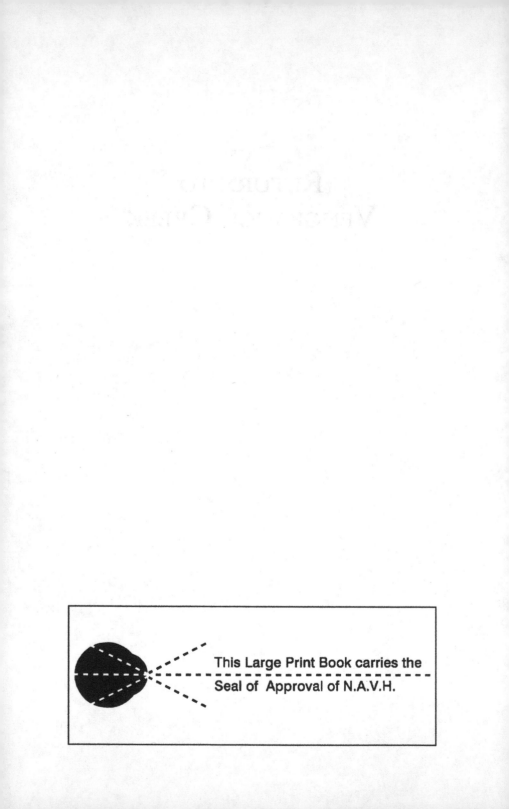

THE SONS OF DANIEL SHAYE

RETURN TO VENGEANCE CREEK

ROBERT J. RANDISI

THORNDIKE PRESS
A part of Gale, a Cengage Company

GALE
A Cengage Company

Farmington Hills, Mich • San Francisco • New York • Waterville, Maine
Meriden, Conn • Mason, Ohio • Chicago

LIBRARY OF CONGRESS CIP DATA ON FILE.
CATALOGUING IN PUBLICATION FOR THIS BOOK
IS AVAILABLE FROM THE LIBRARY OF CONGRESS

ISBN-13: 978-1-4104-9065-0 (hardcover)

Published in 2019 by arrangement with Dominick Abel Literary Agency, Inc.

Printed in Mexico
1 2 3 4 5 6 7 23 22 21 20 19

RETURN TO VENGEANCE CREEK

PROLOGUE

Daniel Shaye reined his horse in just outside the town of Vengeance Creek, Arizona. It was April, but judging by the heat, it could have been August. The town had grown by leaps and bounds since Daniel and his sons were last there. They could see the newest buildings in amongst the more weathered ones, and no doubt there were people in the same conditions.

James and Thomas, Daniel's sons, followed suit, then moved up on either side of him. They had been riding for several days, were ready for hotel beds, baths and café food, not to mention cold beer. But they were also there for a much more important reason.

"You think they'll take us back, Pa?" Thomas asked.

"From what I've heard, they ain't had competent law enforcement here since we left. They'll take us back, all right." Daniel looked at his sons in turn, older Thomas, and then James. "What you boys have to tell me is whether or not you want to be my deputies again."

Now the brothers exchanged a glance, and then Thomas nodded, understanding what had just passed between them.

"Pa, we'll always wanna be your deputies," he told his father. "Ain't that exactly what you raised us for?"

"No, not exactly," Daniel Shaye said. "Your mother would turn over in her grave if that was the case, but it does seem to be turning out that way, doesn't it?"

"We're the Shayes, Pa," James said. "Enforcin' the law is what we do."

"All right, then," Daniel Shaye said, picking up his reins. "Let's get our asses down there and start doin' it!"

ONE

Three months later . . .

Thomas Shaye stood up from the table at the Carver House Café, having just finished a hearty meal. The waitress, a girl named Katrina, came out of the kitchen carrying a tray covered with a red-and-white checkered napkin.

"Here's the food for your prisoners, Tom," she said. "Fried chicken today."

He smiled and accepted the tray from her. "We're not gonna be able to get them to leave. Thanks, Katrina."

"Are you going to the barn dance at the end of the week?" she asked. She was a pretty girl, who had been flirting with him since he and his father and brother had become the law in Vengeance Creek. "I need a partner."

"I'll have to see if I'm gonna be off duty or not," he said. "And I'm afraid I'm not a very good dancer."

9

"Well," she said, folding her arms, "we'll just have to see about that, won't we?"

He returned her smile and left the café.

James Shaye checked the clock on the wall. His brother should be relieving him in five minutes. One thing he could count on with Thomas was that he was always on time. He got that from their late mother. James was more like their father. Daniel Shaye was always ten minutes late, no matter where he was going. But despite that one fault, he was a great lawman.

When they had returned to Vengeance Creek three months earlier, Dan Shaye had presented the mayor and town council with the prospect of once again having himself serve as the local sheriff, and his sons as deputies. It had not taken the mayor long to decide.

They had also gotten themselves a more substantial jail. The adobe building was not brand new, but it had previously been used for storage. Daniel Shaye spotted it and knew that — with the inside reinforced and equipped with a cell block — it would make a perfect jailhouse. Also, it wasn't located dead in the center of town like many sheriffs' offices were, but at a far end and almost outside the town limits.

When the door opened, James saw his

10

brother enter carrying the tray of food and checked the clock.

"Right on time, big brother," he said.

"Our prisoners hungry?"

"Never mind them," James said, "I'm stayin' here."

"Well, little brother, go and get yourself some supper and I'll feed our guests."

James stood up, grabbed his hat from a peg on the wall.

"You see that waitress again?"

"What waitress?" Thomas asked.

"Kathy. The one who's been after you since we got back to town."

"James," Thomas said, "I keep tellin' you we came back here to be the law, not to find ourselves sweethearts or wives."

"Hey," James said, "I ain't lookin' for a wife neither, but a girlfriend or two never hurt nobody."

"Yeah, you tell Pa that," Thomas said, hanging his hat on the vacated peg.

"Where is Pa, anyway?" James asked.

"He said he was havin' supper with the mayor."

"The mayor?" James asked. "Don't tell me Pa's interested in politics."

"You know Pa don't wanna do anythin' but wear a badge," Thomas said, removing the napkin from the top of the tray, reveal-

11

ing two plates of fried chicken. "Naw, he said the mayor had somethin' he wanted to talk about."

"You know," James said, "Mayor Snow was smart enough to hire us back. But I just don't trust him. He's too much of a politician, talkin' outta both sides of his mouth the way he does."

"I know what you mean," Thomas said. He retrieved the keys to the cells from another wall peg.

"He's been givin' in to Pa's requests for three months — like this new jail — but maybe he's about to cash in a chit."

"We'll find out when Pa comes back," Thomas said. "Right now, I ain't gonna worry about it. I gotta feed the prisoners, and you go get yourself some supper. I'll see you later."

"See ya later, big brother," James said, and left.

TWO

The Rawhide Steak House was considered the best place in town to eat. Mayor Abner Snow had a regular table there, and most nights he ate alone. On this night, however, he had a guest for dinner.

Daniel Shaye's salary as sheriff of Vengeance Creek did not allow him to eat in the town's best restaurants very often. Of course, he could have accepted free meals when they were offered, but he refused. He and his boys paid their own ways, were never beholden to anyone, and there were plenty of affordable places in town for them to eat.

Even tonight, however, he did not consider this one of those "free meals." This was a supper with a man who was his boss. And why not let the boss pick up the tab?

"How's your steak, Dan?" Mayor Snow asked. He was a large man in his fifties who

13

indulged most of his appetites on a daily basis.

"It's perfect, Mayor," Shaye said.

"You should eat here more often," Snow said, then raised one hand to ward off Shaye's protest. "I know, I know, you pay your own way. Maybe I can arrange a raise with the town council."

"That'd be real fine, Mayor," Shaye said, "only I'd never be able to accept unless it included my boys."

"Understood, Dan," Snow said, picking up his wine glass. "Understood."

Shaye picked up his beer mug and drank from it, then set it down and went back to work on his thick steak.

"You're probably wondering why I invited you here," Snow said.

"I figured you'd get to it, eventually."

"I took my office just a week after you and your boys left Vengeance Creek . . . the first time."

"Mayor, you know we had to —"

The Mayor waved his hands, cutting off Shaye's protests.

"I understand why you left," Snow said, "and I was happy to rehire you when you came back. There's no problem with any of that."

"Fine," Shaye said, "then keep talkin'."

14

The mayor took another swallow of wine. It was his second glass, and he held it up for the waiter to refill a third time.

"More beer, sir?" the waiter asked Shaye.

"No, thank you." Shaye also had a glass of water, which he'd make do. While he had his badge on, he considered himself on duty. And that was all the time.

The waiter left; the mayor sipped.

"Mayor," Shaye said, "I think you should get to the point before you finish your third glass of wine."

"Oh," Snow said, "uh, yes, of course." He put the glass down. "Ten years ago I was a prosecutor in St. Louis. I spent three years putting men away."

"I think I see where this is going," Shaye said, "but continue."

"I prosecuted a man named Cole Doucette."

"Doucette?" Shaye said, frowning. "I know of a family named Doucette. Hard types. Lawbreakers."

"That's right," Snow said. "There was a father, and uncles, brothers and cousins. Cole's the last one, and he promised he would get me for putting him away."

"That was ten years ago?"

"That's right."

"And have they ever tried?"

15

"Not once."

"But you're thinkin' about them now."

"Yes."

"Why?"

The mayor reached for his glass nervously, then stopped himself and snatched his hand back. Instead, he took out a white handkerchief and mopped the copious perspiration from his face.

"I got Cole Doucette fifteen years inside," he explained. "It was far less than he deserved."

"And?"

The mayor tightened his lips and said, "He's getting out next week."

"What was he put in for?"

"Manslaughter."

"Why's he getting out early?"

The mayor laughed without humor and said, "Good behavior. Can you believe that?"

Shaye studied the mayor's face, then picked up the remainder of his beer and said to Snow, "Have a drink, Mister Mayor."

THREE

Thomas carried the tray of food into the cell block, the keys dangling from one hand.

"Supper, boys!" he announced.

The two prisoners stirred. One had been lying on his back with his arms over his eyes, the other standing at the window, staring out at nothing.

Aaron Boyd rose from the cot and shuffled to the front of the cell to accept his plate through a slot in the door. The skinny nineteen-year-old was still somewhat fuzzy from his drinking the night before, when he had started shooting out some of the crystal lights in the Renegade Saloon & Gambling Hall.

"I'll bring some coffee in a minute," Thomas promised.

"My head still hurts," Boyd complained, sitting on his cot. "You didn't hafta hit me in the head, Deputy."

"It was either that or shoot you, Aaron,"

Thomas said. "Which one would you have voted for?"

Boyd grumbled and bit into a chicken leg.

"What about it, Fleming?" Thomas said. "You want to eat?"

Harry Fleming turned and looked at Thomas. He was a hard-looking twenty-five-year-old who could have passed for forty if he wanted to claim it. He had a sad, sad face.

"I'll take it, Deputy," he said. "I might as well eat while I'm waitin' for my brother. No point in bein' weak from hunger and makin' him have to carry me out — that is, after he kills you."

He walked to the door and accepted the plate with a grin.

"You'd be smart to give your dad that badge and leave town."

"The judge'll be back in two days, Fleming," Thomas said. "Then you'll be out of here and on your way to a federal prison. Murder's like that, you know."

"He's a murderer, and all I did was shoot out a few lights," Boyd complained, "and I gotta be in the cell next to him?"

"Shut yer mouth, kid," Fleming said, "or when my brother comes I'll have him kill you, too."

"Who's this brother yer always talkin'

about?" Boyd asked.

Fleming didn't answer. He had a mouth full of chicken.

"Who is he?" Boyd asked Thomas. "His brother?"

"Fancies himself a gunfighter," Thomas said.

"Ha," Fleming said. "Red Fleming is a gunfighter. He's the fastest gun around."

"There ain't no more gunfighters, Fleming," Thomas said. "Those days are long gone."

"Wait a minute," Boyd said, licking his fingers. "Red Fleming. I've heard that name."

"See?" Fleming said. "He's heard of my brother. Everybody has. He's killed ten men."

"Your little brother, right?" Thomas said.

"He's thirty-five," Fleming said.

"And he's out there while you're in jail?" Boyd asked. "Sounds like he's the one with the talent."

"Yeah, well, we're a team."

"He's the fast gun," Thomas said, "and what're you?"

"Me," Fleming said around a mouthful of mashed potatoes, "I'm the brains."

"Oh, right," Thomas said. "Why didn't I

guess that? Call me when you guys finish eating."

He left the cell block.

Boyd looked at Fleming.

"My brother's gonna kill 'im," Fleming said. "Them Shayes, they got a reputation — especially the old man."

"So why's he gonna kill the deputy?" Boyd asked. "Why not the sheriff?"

"The deputy's the one who put me in here," Fleming said. "He's the one's gonna pay."

"And then the sheriff and his other son will come after you and your brother."

"I don't care," Fleming said. "Red will kill them, too. And then we'll have a huge reputation."

"You?" Boyd asked. "You mean your brother will."

"Like I said," Fleming replied, "we're a team."

Boyd shook his head and went back to his dinner.

"So what do you want me to do, Mayor?" Dan Shaye asked over coffee and pie. "Track him down? Once he's out, he's a free man. He hasn't done anythin'. And I can't just leave town —"

"No, no," Mayor Snow said. "I just wanted

20

to let you know that Cole Doucette and his family might be coming here looking for me sometime in the future."

"Hopefully," Shaye said, "it'll be in the far future."

"Right, right," Snow said. "Maybe they won't ever come. Maybe Doucette has even forgotten about me after all these years."

"Yeah," Shaye said, "maybe." He knew how families were. They never forgot a slight, or a debt. He knew that much from experience. And western families, they were the worst. And Cole, being the last, would feel duty bound to keep a promise like that.

Daniel Shaye had put many men in jail over the years, and he knew that none of them had forgotten about him, at all. When someone takes away years of your life, you tend to remember that person — but he didn't bother telling the mayor that.

The mayor took care of the bill and the two men walked outside.

"How are you and your boys getting on?" Snow asked. "With the job, I mean."

"No problem," Shaye said. "We've done this before. Thomas takes to it naturally. He's like me."

"And James?"

"I still think James should go back East to school," Shaye said. "Maybe become a

21

lawyer." He realized that would only make the mayor think about what they'd been discussing, so he quickly added, "Or a doctor, maybe. He's gentler, like his Ma. Looks more like her, too."

"He is a bright lad," Snow said. "Anybody can see that."

"Thomas is smart, too," Shaye said, "just in a different way."

"You've got good boys, Dan," Snow said, slapping the lawman on the back. "Good boys."

When the mayor walked off, Shaye had no idea if the man was going back to work or home. He'd had so much wine, Shaye hoped he was going home.

FOUR

On his way to the jailhouse, Dan Shaye ran into his son James.

"Aren't you supposed to be eating?" he asked.

"I had a sandwich," James said. "I want to get back to the jail."

"Isn't Thomas there?"

"Yes."

"Then you can go home."

The town had included a house with three bedrooms when they hired the Shayes to be their law.

"What's at home?" James asked. "I'd much rather be at the jail with you and Thomas."

Shaye noticed that James's deputy badge had a high sheen on it. More than once he'd come into the office and found the boy polishing the silver star. He was never going to get James to go to college as long as he loved wearing a badge that much.

23

"What did the mayor want," James asked, "that was worth him buying you supper?"

"Come on," Shaye said. "I'll tell you and your brother at the same time."

When they entered the adobe jailhouse, Thomas looked up at them from behind the desk. He had his feet up and was leafing through wanted posters.

"What are you doin' here?" he asked his brother. "Ain't your badge shiny enough?"

James looked down at his badge and quickly ran his cuff over it.

"Never mind that," Shaye said. "Have a seat, James, and get out of my chair, Thomas."

"Sure, Pa." Thomas dropped his feet to the floor and stood up. Shaye walked around and sat, moving the stack of posters to the side while his boys pulled up chairs.

"What's goin' on?" Thomas asked.

"Pa's gonna tell us what the mayor wanted," James explained.

"He's a politician," Thomas said. "What else could he want but votes?"

"Not quite," Shaye said. "He's got a little problem he wanted to let us know about."

"Us?" Thomas asked.

"That's right." He went on to tell his sons about Cole Doucette and the whole Doucette clan.

24

"You ever heard of the Doucettes, Pa?"

"Once or twice," Shaye said. "Never ran into them, though."

"So you think they're comin' here?" James asked.

"Don't know," Shaye said. "Cole's the last, and I told the mayor I'd look into it."

"How you gonna do that?" James asked.

"I'll send some telegrams," Shaye said. "To the prison and some lawmen I know, see what anybody's heard."

"Other than that," Thomas said, "seems to me all we got to do is wait for Doucette to get here."

"If they're comin', at all," James added. He looked at Shaye. "Who says they even are, right, Pa?"

"They're comin' all right, James."

"But how do you know?"

"When a man puts you in jail," his father said, "you don't forget it."

"Yeah, but maybe he knows he deserved it," James suggested. "What about that?"

"That ain't likely, little brother," Thomas said. "We just gotta face that they'll be here sooner or later."

James looked from his brother back to his father.

"How many of 'em?"

"Now, that we won't know till they get

25

here," Shaye said.

"Then what do we do?"

"We make sure we're ready for them, James," Shaye said.

"Do we hire more deputies?"

"Maybe," Shaye said, "we'll have to wait and see."

Thomas made a rude noise with his mouth and said, "Not likely."

"What do you mean?" James asked.

"This is what folks hire us for, James," Thomas said. "You ain't about to get these storekeepers out on the streets with a gun and a badge."

"Pa?" James said.

"It's like I already said," Shaye relied, "we'll just have to wait and see what happens." He looked at Thomas. "Did you feed the prisoners?"

"Yes, sir," he said. "I just have to go in and get the dirty plates."

"I'll do that," Shaye said. "You can go and make your rounds. And you," he said to his younger son, "go home and get some rest."

"But Pa —"

"That's an order, Deputy."

"Yessir."

Shaye sat back in his chair and watched his two boys walk through the front door, chattering at each other, as usual. Times

26

like this, when the boys were together, made him think of his third son Matthew, killed by Ethan Langer. Langer had also killed Dan Shaye's wife when Shaye was the sheriff of Epitaph, Texas. He and the boys had hunted down the Langer gang, and as a result, Langer had killed Matthew — his middle son — and Thomas had killed Langer.

They'd come to Vengeance Creek, Arizona, after that, tried to settle down and enforce the law again, but after tracking down a gang of bank robbers, Shaye had decided that ranching might be safer for his boys. He bought a place outside of Winchester, Wyoming, but that didn't last. A letter about a possible grandson took them to Pearl River Junction to see if Matthew had, indeed, left behind a baby boy. By the time they found out the story was bogus, there was nothing left for them but to take up the badge, again. Shaye had been sure Vengeance Creek would take them back, and he was right. The new mayor had jumped at the chance to have them.

Maybe now he knew the real reason why.

FIVE

Shaye got up to go into the cell block and collect the dirty plates. The kid, Boyd, was on his back as usual, and his breathing indicated he was asleep. Balanced in the slot was his meal plate, along with the spoon that had been given him. The prisoners were not allowed forks or knives.

Shaye grabbed the plate, moved on to the next cell.

Fleming was sitting on his cot, looking very calm. His plate was next to him.

"Let me have that plate, Fleming," Shaye said.

"Sure, Sheriff." He got up, handed Shaye the plate and spoon, and then sat back down. "You know your boy don't have long to live, don't you?" he asked.

"That right?"

"Yep," Fleming said. "My brother Red'll be here soon. He's already killed ten men, so one more deputy ain't gonna make a difference."

"What I heard about your brother is that he shot most of those men in the back," Shaye said.

Fleming's face darkened.

"You shouldn't oughtta say that, Sheriff. I'm just warnin' ya to watch out for your family. My brother and me, we watch out for each other."

"Don't you worry about my family, Fleming. If your brother is stupid enough to come to town tryin' to break you out and goes up against my boy, Thomas will take care of business."

"You three Shayes," Fleming said, shaking his head, "you better not gang up on my brother. That ain't a fair fight."

"Don't worry, Fleming," Shaye said. "We'll do what it takes to uphold the law."

Fleming was still shouting threats as Shaye left the cell block with the plates, pulling the door closed behind him.

"Why don't I do your rounds with you?" James said to Thomas outside.

"Why don't you do what Pa tells you to do for once?" Thomas replied. "Just go home and get some sleep."

"I'm not sleepy."

"Then go home and have a whiskey and

relax," Thomas said.

"What do you think about this Doucette family coming to town?" James asked.

"I think we took care of the Langers when we had to," Thomas said, "and we'll take care of the Doucettes, the Flemings, and any other families who wanna come after us, because we're the family that counts."

"The Flemings?" James asked. "But —"

"Go home, James!" Thomas said, and set off to make his late rounds.

By morning, Thomas and James came out of their rooms to the smell of breakfast from the kitchen and found their dad at the stove flipping flapjacks. They shared a house the town had given them as part of the job.

"Sit," Shaye said. "Gonna make you boys a nice breakfast to start the day."

"What brought this on?" James asked, sitting at the table.

"I just felt like havin' your momma's flapjacks today," Shaye said, putting a plate on the table with a large stack on it. "Dig in."

Over breakfast James asked Thomas, "What'd you mean last night about the Fleming family?"

"Aw, it's nothin'," Thomas said.

"Pa?"

"The prisoner claims his brother, Red Fleming, is some kind of fast gun. Says he's gonna come to town to get him out, and kill your brother for puttin' him in jail."

"How come everybody's got a father or brother or an uncle who fancies themselves a fast gun?" James asked.

"That's the way it was in the old days," Shaye said. "You had the James boys, and the Youngers, the Earps and the Mastersons . . . lottsa families with reputations."

"Like ours," Thomas said. "Pa here is a famous lawman."

"And what about us?" James asked.

Thomas laughed. "Come on, little brother. Nobody knows who the hell we are."

"Maybe they will, some day."

Thomas pointed his knife at his brother and said, "Maybe if you went back East to law school or somethin', that'd be true."

James returned the gesture with his own knife and said, "Don't start that again!"

"I'm just sayin' —"

"Pa —"

"Both of you just shut up and eat," Daniel Shaye said. "Let's just keep our minds on the job at hand. Thomas, we gotta release the Boyd kid, today. His Pa's gonna pay for damages."

"Suits me."

"And Fleming?" James asked.

"Still waitin' for the judge," Shaye said.

"Or Red Fleming," James said.

"Whoever," Shaye said.

"Pa, does this Red Fleming have a reputation?"

"I've heard somethin' about him."

"Then you ain't gonna let Thomas face him alone, are you?"

"Don't you worry about me," Thomas said. "I ain't afraid to face no wanna-be gunfighter."

"Let's not go lookin' for trouble, boys," Shaye said. "We'll just handle what comes along when it comes along. Now finish up, and then go clean up."

"Ma never made us clean up," James said.

"I ain't your ma," Shaye said.

"From the taste of these flapjacks," Thomas said, "that's more than true."

SIX

When they got to the jailhouse, they relieved Harvey Ludlow, a man who did odd jobs in town. When the saloon needed swamping, or the livery stable needed sweeping, or the jail needed to be watched, Harvey was your man.

As they entered, Harvey stood up. He was six-and-a-half feet tall and couldn't have weighed more than 130 pounds soaking wet.

"Okay, thanks for givin' me a break, Harvey," Shaye said.

"Sure, Sheriff," Harvey said. "Any time."

"Any trouble?"

"No, sir," Harvey said. "Your prisoners were real quiet."

"Go to the café. I arranged for them to give you breakfast. They won't charge you."

The young man smiled broadly and said, "Thanks, Sheriff! See you, boys."

" 'Bye, Harvey," James said.

Harvey left, and Shaye sat behind his desk.

"Okay, you boys go out and do your mornin' rounds," Shaye said. "I'll wait for Katrina to get here with the prisoners' breakfasts."

"She's gonna be real disappointed not to find Thomas here," James said, with a grin. "That girl's got her sights set on you. How about a spring weddin'? Sound good?"

"Shut up, James," Thomas said.

"Go!" Shaye said. "Fight outside."

Thomas and James went out the door, still bickering. Only when the door closed behind them did their father smile.

Red Fleming sat at the campfire and drank his coffee. Around him, his men were breaking camp, dousing their fires and saddling their horses.

"We're almost ready, Red," Dan Cannaday told him. Everyone called him "Candy." Even on his wanted poster it said Dan "Candy" Cannaday.

Red dumped the remainder of his coffee into the fire, said to Candy, "Have somebody douse that one," and handed him the cup.

"Bentley," Candy shouted, "douse this fire!"

"Right!"

Candy turned and followed Red, who

walked to his horse and began to saddle it.

"We gettin' this done today?" Candy asked.

"We are."

Red, at thirty-five, was about eight years older than Candy, who recognized not only Red's ability with a gun, but his leadership qualities. He had no problem being Number Two to the older man . . . for now.

"What about the town?" Candy asked.

"What about it?" Red asked.

"What do we do to it after we get your brother out of jail?"

Red dropped his blanket onto his horse's back, then turned to face Candy. He had black hair and black stubble on his face. "Red" was not a nickname, it was what his parents named him.

"What are you talkin' about?" he demanded. "You wanna burn the town down after? Loot it? Rape the women?"

"All of it," Candy said, licking his lips.

Red looked around at the other five men in camp.

"They feel the same way?"

"Pretty much."

"That's not why I'm goin' to Vengeance Creek," Red told him. "Never was."

"I know," Candy said. "You're goin' to get your brother out of jail. Keep him from hangin'."

"That's right. I ain't no town-burner, Candy."

He bent over, lifted his saddle and tossed it up onto his horse's back.

"So then, what's in it for us?" Candy asked. "The rest of us? You said you'd make it worth our while to help you break your brother out."

"And I will," Red said. "Me and my brother, we both will. But you burn down that town, and we'll be runnin' for the rest of our lives. Especially if you rape the women and kill all the men. The law has a way of not forgettin' about things like that."

"But this way you and your brother are gonna make it worth stickin' our necks out," Candy said. "None of it's legal, is it?"

"No."

"So the law will still be after us."

"Maybe," Red said, "but it ain't gonna be for mass murder."

"Mass murder?"

"That's what they'd call it."

"So whatta you gonna do? Break your brother out and kill a lawman?"

"Just one," Red said. "The one who put him in there."

"Ain't that murder?"

Red turned to face Candy again.

"Not if it's a fair fight, my friend," Red said. "Right out in the center of the street."

"You think you're Wild Bill Hickok, don't ya?" Candy asked.

"Not Hickok," Red said, "just me, Red Fleming. Now, you better get saddled up."

"Okay," Candy said, "but I ain't convinced about this, and I don't know if the others will be, either."

"Well," Red said, putting his left hand on Candy's shoulder and looking him square in the eye, "I'll just have to convince you, and then you and me, we'll convince them."

"I been to Vengeance Creek once or twice before, ya know," Candy said.

"So?"

"That town would burn real good," Candy said, shaking his head. "Real good."

"Well then," Red Fleming said, "another time, maybe."

SEVEN

It was later in the day when Red Fleming rode into town with his men.

"I want the street to be busy," he explained to Candy. "Nobody'll start shootin' with innocent bystanders on the street."

"Except maybe us," Candy said, with a laugh.

"Except maybe us," Red agreed.

But they didn't start shooting. Not as soon as they rode in.

Daniel Shaye was in his office, wondering whether he should have lunch there or actually get over to the café to eat. He'd make the decision when Thomas relieved him.

Thomas was already at the café, sitting alone in a corner, eating his lunch and trading flirtatious remarks with Katrina.

It was James who was on the street as the Fleming gang rode in. He saw the men, because James always kept a sharp eye out for trouble, and this many men riding into town together was a definite portent of trouble.

James backed into some equipment outside of the hardware store, using it to watch the group as they rode past, hoping they didn't notice him. Could this have been Red Fleming, come to town to free his brother from jail? Or was it the family the mayor was worried about, the Doucettes? Or was this something totally different, just a bunch of cowboys looking to blow off a little steam?

He continued to watch the riders after they rode by him and, as expected, they reined in their horses in front of the Renegade Saloon.

Once he saw them dismount and go inside, he stepped away from the hardware store and headed for the sheriff's office.

"Riders just came in, Pa," James said, as soon as he entered the office.

"How many?"

"Six or seven."

"Which is it, James?"

James hesitated, then said, "Seven."

Dan Shaye stood up, grabbed his hat and gunbelt from a rack on the wall.

"Where's your brother? Still at the café?"

"As far as I know? Who d'ya think they

are, Pa?"

"Could be anybody," Shaye said, "but we're gonna find out for sure, boy. Where'd they go?"

"The Renegade."

"Let's go get your brother," Shaye said, heading for the door.

"Should we, Pa?"

Shaye stopped. "Why not?"

"What if it's Red Fleming?"

"What if it is?"

"Harry says his brother Red is gonna kill Thomas."

"You said there's seven men."

"That's right."

"Well, whether it's Red Fleming or not, we're better off with the three of us than just two, don't ya think?"

"Well . . . sure, but —"

"No buts," Shaye said. "Let's go and get your brother."

Thomas was, indeed, still in the café. He was drinking coffee and eating a hunk of pie while Katrina sat across from him. There were only two other customers in the place, a married couple still working on their lunches, so Katrina sat with her chin in her hand, watching Thomas chew.

"Look how happy they are," she said.

"Who?"

"Mr. and Mrs. Horton, right there."

Thomas looked over at the middle-aged couple, who each seemed to be concentrating on their own meal.

"They're not even talkin' to each other," he said.

"They don't have to," Katrina said. "They're that connected. Don't you think you could ever be that connected with a woman, Thomas?"

"I don't care how connected you are, Katrina," Thomas said, "you still gotta talk, some time."

"Well, I'm sure they do, but what I meant was —"

"This was really good pie, Kat," Thomas said, pushing his empty plate away. "Can I get some more coffee?"

Frustrated, the waitress stood up and said, "Of course," but before she could go to the kitchen for the pot, Sheriff Daniel Shaye walked in, followed by Deputy James.

"Thomas, let's go," Shaye said.

"What's goin' on, Pa?"

"Some men just rode into town. Might be Red Fleming."

Thomas stood up.

"If it is, he must be lookin' for me."

"He might be lookin' for you, brother,"

James sad, "but he's going to find all of us."

"Pa," Thomas said, "you gotta let me handle this."

"Son," Shaye said, "Fleming's got six men with him. You ready to go up against seven men?"

"No," Thomas had to admit.

"Then let's go," his father said. "We do this the way we do most things — together."

Thomas looked at Katrina, who was standing by, looking worried.

"How much do I owe you, Kat?"

"Nothin', Thomas," she said. "Just go . . . and don't get yourself killed!" She looked at Daniel and James. "Any of you."

"We won't, Miss Katrina," Shaye said.

"Where are they?" Thomas asked his brother as they went out the front door.

"At the Renegade."

"Pa?" Thomas said. "Maybe we should give them some time to get a little liquored up, first."

"That's a good idea, son," Shaye said. "Whiskey might make 'em short tempered, and they won't be seein' straight."

EIGHT

In the Renegade Saloon, Red Fleming and his six men were lined up at the bar. Fleming and Candy were off to one side, while the other five men stood at the other end, laughing and drinking.

"Gimme another drink," Fleming said to the bartender.

The man came over with a bottle and filled his shot glass. Fleming reached out and grabbed the bartender's arm.

"Leave the bottle."

"Yeah, sure," the bartender said, and put it down.

"Red," Candy asked, "when are we gonna go look for some Shayes?"

"We ain't," Fleming said. "They're gonna find us." He pushed the bottle toward Candy. "Have another."

"You wanna be drunk when they find us?" Candy asked.

"I don't get drunk when I drink," Red

43

Fleming said. "I get faster."

"What about them?" Candy asked, indicating the other men.

"They'll get drunk," Fleming said, "and then dead."

"So you're willin' to sacrifice them to get your brother out of jail?"

"Every last one of 'em."

"And me?"

"No," Fleming said. "Of course not you, Candy."

Candy studied Fleming's profile as the man stared into his own whiskey glass, then pushed the bottle away.

When the Shayes reached the saloon, Daniel stopped and peered over the tops of the batwing doors.

"There's a group of men at the bar," he said to his sons. "Take a look, James."

He moved aside so James could take his place.

"That's them," James said. "Those are the men I saw ride in. Is one of 'em Red Fleming?"

"I don't know," Shaye said, "but let's find out." He turned to Thomas. "Don't draw unless I do."

"Okay."

Then, remembering that his son was faster

44

than he was, he added, "Unless it becomes absolutely necessary."

"Got it."

Thomas and James bookended their father and the three of them entered the saloon.

Red Fleming had been watching the batwings in the mirror behind the bar. When the lawmen walked in, he wasn't surprised. He nudged Candy, who looked over his shoulder, then moved down to the men at the end of the bar.

"Okay," he said, "it's time for you fellas to earn your money."

"Those three?" one asked.

"Yep."

"They don't look like much."

"Just do your jobs," Candy said, and moved back toward Red as the lawmen approached the bar.

"Red Fleming?"

One of the men turned as Shaye said his name.

"Can I help you, Sheriff?"

"Shaye," the lawman said, "my name's Sheriff Shaye. These are my deputies —"

"And your sons," Fleming finished. "Yeah, I heard of you."

"Then you've also heard that we have your

45

brother in our jail."

"Oh, yeah. I heard."

Thomas noticed that Fleming's gun was on his left hip, and his whiskey glass was in his right hand. It was standard practice for a gunman to leave his gunhand free.

"So, is that why you came to town?" Shaye asked. "To break him out?"

"We came to town to have some drinks," the man said. "That's all. Breaking into your jail, that would be against the law. We don't break the law. Ain't that right, boys?"

"That's right, boss," one of them said, and the others nodded and laughed. "We never break the law."

"Wouldn't even think of it," another said.

"So why don't you lawmen go and shoot a stray dog or somethin'," a third man said, causing more laughter.

James bristled. "Tell me, if I go back to the office and look through our wanted posters, what will I find? Pictures of any of you, maybe?"

"And what if you did?" the man who mentioned the stray dog asked. "What would the three of you do to the six of us, huh?"

"Wait a minute," Shaye said, looking at his sons. "Six?"

"What?" James asked.

"There were seven men when we came in," Shaye said. "Now there's six."

"You're right," Thomas said.

"What are you talkin' about?" the man who answered to Red Fleming's name demanded.

"You're not Fleming," Shaye said.

"The jail!" Thomas said. "Damn!"

"Wait a minute!" the false Fleming — actually Candy — said.

"Go!" Shaye shouted to Thomas.

Thomas turned and ran for the door.

"Hold it!" Candy yelled.

"Go for that gun and we're gonna have some big problems," Shaye said to Candy.

The other five men were fidgety now, watching Candy for a signal.

Candy, on the other hand, was calming down. Fleming hadn't said anything about getting into a shoot-out with the law. He just wanted to get his brother out of jail.

"Okay, hold on, now," he said to Shaye. "Nobody said anythin' about goin' for their guns."

"No," Shaye said, "you were just supposed to keep us busy here long enough for Fleming to get his brother out."

Candy didn't answer. He held his hand up to the other men, to keep them from doing something stupid.

"If somethin' bad happens in my jail," Shaye said, "you're all gonna pay for it."

"Well then," one of the other men said, "maybe we should just go for our guns, huh, Candy?"

NINE

Thomas ran through town, intent on getting to the jailhouse as soon as possible — hopefully in time to keep Red Fleming from breaking his brother out of jail. The only person there to stop him was the odd job man, Harvey Ludlow.

He got to the jail and burst through the front door, drawing his gun as he went. He needn't have bothered. It was quiet. Nothing seemed amiss, but that didn't necessarily mean anything. He moved slowly toward the door to the cell block, peered inside, saw that none of the cells had open doors. Maybe he had somehow beaten Red Fleming there.

He entered the block, noticing a form on the cot in Harry Fleming's cell — but he was sure it wasn't Fleming.

"Ah, no," he said, opening the door and rushing into the cell. He grabbed the man and turned him over. It was Harvey, and he was dead, stabbed.

"Damn it, Harvey."

He left the cell, ran to the back door of the jailhouse and out into the alley. It was deserted, but there in the dirt were the tracks of two horses. Red Fleming had killed Harvey, and gotten away with his brother, Harry.

Thomas ran back through the jailhouse, hurrying back up the street toward the saloon.

As Shaye and James exited the saloon, leaving Candy and the other Fleming men inside, they saw Thomas running toward them.

"What happened?" Shaye asked.

"Fleming," Thomas said, out of breath. "He killed Harvey and got his brother out. They're gone."

"Harvey's dead?" James said, shocked.

The three Shayes stood there for a moment in silence.

"He used all that talk about him bein' a fast gun to outsmart me," Shaye finally said.

"He outsmarted all of us," James said.

"What about these others?" Thomas asked. "Do you think they know where he's goin'?"

"Probably not," Shaye said, "but there's

that one, called Candy . . . Let's go back inside and ask."

They went into the Renegade and saw five men still standing at the bar. The sixth man, Candy, was gone.

"Okay, boys," Shaye said, "new plan."

The men turned to look at Shaye and his sons.

"You again?"

"I want you to put your guns on the bar," Shaye said. "Hold them with two fingers, please."

The men didn't move, but they also didn't have Candy to look to for guidance.

"It's five to three now, fellas," Thomas said. "You can't like the odds."

For a moment Thomas thought the men would go for their guns, but one by one they laid their pistols and rifles on the bar, holding them with two fingers.

"Bartender," Shaye said, "collect that iron before somebody gets brave, please, and stow it below the bar."

"Yessir," the bartender said. He gathered all the guns and quickly removed them from the bar.

"Okay," Shaye said, "now we can talk without anybody gettin' stupid. You." He pointed to one man, the one who'd made the comment about the stray dog. "What's your name?"

"Bentley."

"Okay, Bentley," Shaye said, "where was your boss goin' after he broke his brother out?"

"I dunno," the man said. "He didn't tell us stuff like that."

"We was just a distraction," another man said.

"And you already got paid?" Thomas asked.

Bentley nodded.

"What about Candy?" Shaye asked.

"He went out the back after you went out the front," Bentley said.

"Is he goin' to meet the Flemings?" Shaye asked.

"Probably," Bentley said. "He's been ridin' with them a long time."

"And he never said where they were goin'?"

"Never," Bentley said. "Red would kill him if he talked."

Shaye exchanged a glance with each of his boys, then looked at the men again.

"Okay," Shaye said, "your visit to Vengeance Creek is officially over. I want you all out of town within the hour."

"What about our guns?" one man asked.

"You'll get them back as you ride out,"

Shaye said, "unloaded. Try the north end."

He turned to leave, and his sons followed.

"What do we do now?" Thomas asked when they got outside.

"I should put together a posse," Shaye said, "but that'll take time."

"And all I have to do is saddle my horse," Thomas said.

"Do a little more than that, Thomas," Shaye said. "Outfit yourself. It may take you a few days, or longer, to track them."

"Right. What about you?"

"I have to stay in town," Shaye said. "I told the mayor I'd be here if and when Cole Doucette comes to town."

"Okay, then," Thomas said. "You two be careful."

"And you," James said, looking concerned.

Thomas ran off down the street toward the livery.

"Pa, don't you think I should go with him?" James asked, turning to his father.

"No," Shaye said, putting his hand on his son's shoulder. "I've got another job for you."

"What?"

"Thomas is gonna track the Flemings," Shaye said. "I want you to track Candy."

"But . . . how? I'm no tracker."

"You know what I've taught you, James,"

Shaye said. "Candy went out the back door. That means he must have had a horse there."

"Okay," James said. "So Thomas has to track the two Flemings alone, and I leave you here to face Cole Doucette by yourself."

"With any luck at all," Shaye said, "Candy will lead you to the Flemings and Thomas. Together, you'll be able to take them."

"And you?" James asked. "What if Doucette gets here with a gang? And what if the mayor's just jumpin' at shadows, and Cole Doucette's not comin' here at all?"

"Look, son, that's a chance we'll have to take," Shaye said.

"But Pa —"

"I made the mayor a promise. So go saddle your horse."

"Yessir."

James knew better than to argue when his father had his mind set on something.

TEN

Shaye claimed the surrendered weapons from the bartender, then waited at the north end of town. As the gang rode by, he gave them each their weapon.

"Don't come back to town," he told them.

"We wouldn't think of it, Sheriff," Bentley said.

Shaye watched them ride away and wished he had one more deputy to send after them, to trail them. He had a feeling Bentley was a long time *compadre* of the Fleming boys. But he was going to have to leave it to his sons to find Red and Harry.

Once the Fleming men were gone, Shaye walked back to the center of town and entered City Hall. It was the newest building in Vengeance Creek, a two-story brick structure that would also house the Vengeance Creek Police Department if the mayor ever got the town council to approve it. Shaye knew this, but hadn't shared the information with his sons. Not yet, anyway.

A police department was in the distant — well, maybe not so distant — future, but certainly not something to worry about yet. He was there to talk to the mayor, whose office was on the second floor.

As he entered the outer office a middle-aged woman, seated at a desk, looked up and smiled. Agatha Helmund was a part-time employee of the city, working as a receptionist for the mayor when she wasn't working in Miss Mitzi's Dress Shop. She was a widow, so both jobs kept her fairly busy and away from her empty home.

"Good afternoon, Sheriff."

"Agatha," he greeted. Upon their initial meeting, she had insisted he call her by her first name. "Not so good, I'm afraid. Is he in?"

"He is, but he's left instructions not to be disturbed unless it's an emergency."

"I believe this qualifies," he said. "Harvey Ludlow's been killed."

"Oh, my!" she said. "Oh, my goodness." She slid her chair back. "I'll tell him you're here." She stood, turned to walk away, then turned back. "H-how did he — I mean, how was he killed?"

"I think I should tell the mayor that before I tell you, Agatha," Shaye said.

56

"Yes, yes, of course you must," she said. "I'm sure he'll see you."

She went to the door of the mayor's office, knocked and entered. In moments she returned, leaving the door open behind her.

"You can go in, Sheriff."

"Thank you, Agatha."

Shaye entered the office and Agatha closed the door behind him. Mayor Abner Snow stood behind his huge desk, looking alarmed.

"What the hell happened to Harvey, Sheriff?" he demanded, brusquely.

"It was Red Fleming, Mayor," Shaye said. "He broke his brother out of jail and killed Harvey in the process."

"And where were you and your deputies when this happened?" Snow demanded.

"We were in the Renegade, facing down the rest of his men," Shaye said.

"I didn't hear any gunfire."

"There was none," Shaye sad. "Harvey was stabbed, and we dispatched Fleming's other men without firing any shots. He simply used them to distract us. I'm afraid I was . . . snookered," Shaye said, embarrassed.

Snow sat heavily behind his desk and waved at Shaye to sit also.

"Where are your boys, Sheriff?"

"They're tracking the Fleming brothers," Shaye said, seating himself.

"Without you?"

"They're very capable, Mayor," Shaye said. "Besides, I promised you I'd be here in case Cole Doucette showed up, didn't I?"

"I'm glad to hear that," the mayor said. "I'm sorry about Harvey, and I'm sure your boys will drag Harry Fleming back here to stand trial. But I got this today, first thing in the morning." He picked up a telegram from his desk.

"What's that?"

"I put the word out on Cole Doucette," the mayor said. "This telegram says he's headed in this direction."

"But does it say he's actually comin' here?"

"It doesn't say that," Snow replied, "but why else would he be coming this way?"

"I guess we'll find out soon enough," Shaye said. "How far away does it put him?"

"In New Mexico," the mayor said. "If he keeps coming, he could be here in four or five days."

"Well then," Shaye said, standing, "I guess we'll just have to wait and see, won't we?"

"I think we have to do more than that," Snow said.

"Whataya mean?"

"It also says he's got some men with him."

"How many?"

"I don't know exactly, but since you sent both of your deputies out to chase down the Fleming brothers, maybe you better hire some new ones."

"Do you think I can just pin some tin on a few shirts and have deputies?" Shaye asked. "Men who'll be able to face up to Cole Doucette in four days?"

"I don't know, Sheriff," Mayor Snow said. "I guess that would depend on how fast and how well you can train them. Or maybe what you need to do is find men who can already handle a gun."

"I'm not about to pin some badge on a couple of hired guns, Mr. Mayor," Shaye said. "If Cole Doucette really does arrive here, you're just gonna have to leave it to me how we handle him. After all, that's what you asked me to do."

Shaye turned and headed for the door.

"Dan," Mayor Snow said, "Doucette's not about to hesitate to go through you to get to me."

"Well," Shaye said, "that's just somethin' else we'll have to see about, ain't it?"

Eleven

In their haste to get away from Vengeance Creek, the Flemings did nothing to try to hide their tracks. This made it fairly easy for Thomas to trail them — at least, in the beginning.

Dan Shaye was the best tracker Thomas had ever known, and his father had taught him everything he could. So when the tracks disappeared into a stream, he knew he didn't just have two options — upstream or downstream — but that he had *both* options. He was going to have to pick one, and if he chose wrong, then he'd have to retrace his steps and go the other way. If that was the case, the Flemings would be able to put more miles between themselves and him.

He sat his horse and took a moment to make up his mind. He knew the nearest town was called Forsythe, to the north. The question was, did the Flemings know that?

And since they were on the run, would they ride to the nearest town or away from it? He decided that if he was on the run, he'd go south — downstream — away from Forsythe, which had its own sheriff. By now his Pa might have sent out some telegrams, warning nearby towns about the Flemings.

He finally decided to stop putting so much thought into it, and simply turned his horse south and began riding.

Harry Fleming grumbled almost the entire ride away from Vengeance Creek.

"I don't understand why we're not going to Forsythe, Red," he complained.

"That's why I'm in charge and you're not, Harry," Red said. "The posse that's after us is gonna expect us to go to Forsythe. It's the closest town to Vengeance Creek. They'd expect us to go there to get outfitted."

"So if we ain't goin' there, where are we gonna get outfitted then?"

"We're headed for an old line shack I know about," Red said. "It's only about five more miles. I got supplies waitin' for us there. Once we pick them up, we'll be on our way outta Arizona."

"Wait," Harry said, reining in his horse abruptly. "We ain't goin' back to Vengeance Creek to burn it down?"

Red rode a few feet farther before stopping and turning his horse.

"Why the hell would we do that?"

"Well . . . they put me in jail!" Harry complained. "They was gonna hang me, Red! You gonna let 'em get away with that?"

"You killed a man, Harry," Red said, "and you got caught. What did you think they was gonna do with ya? Pin a medal on your chest?"

"Look," the younger Fleming brother said, "if there's a posse after us, then the town ain't got no protection. We can just go back —"

"Harry," Red said, holding his hand up, "just stop talkin', will ya? The more you talk, the dumber you sound. Once we get outta Arizona, ain't no posse gonna be followin' us."

"Yeah, but . . . I'm gonna be wanted."

"We're already wanted in two other states, brother," Red said. "That's why we're goin' to Ol' Mexico."

"Mexico?"

"That's right," Red said. "Now, just follow me and shut up."

He turned his horse and began riding. Harry sat there for a few seconds, then spurred his horse on and shouted, "But all they eat in Mexico is beans. I hate beans!"

■ ■ ■ ■

James knew he'd never be the tracker his father was. Hell, he'd never be as good as Thomas, either. But this fella Candy didn't seem to be doing anything to cover his tracks. Either he was stupid, in too much of a rush, or he wanted to be followed. If he was stupid or in a rush, James had to keep following. If he wanted to be followed, it meant he was leading James away from the Fleming brothers.

He decided he had only one option, and that was to keep following. If he could catch up to the man, he might be able to convince him to tell him where the Flemings were headed. Thomas was on their trail alone, and for all they knew the two Flemings were on their way to meet the rest of the men. James knew how good his older brother was with a gun, but against a gang he'd need help.

James pushed his mount whenever he could, especially when the trail was very clear, but there were times he had to walk the horse, so he could study the ground. Whether Candy was trying or not, sometimes the terrain simply made it hard to read any sign. Then, when he found it again, he could once again push on. But there was a lot of stop and go involved. Eventually it started to get dark, and he knew he had to make camp.

Candy rode hell-bent-for-leather out of Vengeance Creek. His instructions were clear. Leave a trail that was easy to read, ride for about fifty miles, and then double back and meet Red and Harry Fleming in Mexico. But fifty miles would fill a day, and he knew he was going to have to camp for the night. What he wanted to do, though, was cover the mileage, double back, and then camp. That way no lawman dumb enough to keep moving at night would stumble over him in the dark.

TWELVE

Shaye was in the Renegade Saloon that night, nursing a beer, thinking about Harvey's death and sending his boys out after the killers. It was the first time James had gone out on his own. Thomas had been out before, but only two or three times, and certainly never to track two killers. He probably should have gone with James, but that would have left the town with no lawman.

He had to balance his responsibilities as a father with his duties as a peace officer. And there he had to take into consideration the fact that his sons were now grown men. He couldn't be with them all the time, every step of the way; not anymore. Thomas had already proven himself, but this would be a good test for James, to determine if he should really be wearing a badge.

He was finishing his beer when the batwings opened and the mayor stepped in, followed by two men wearing dour expressions and low-slung guns. Not a good combination.

The mayor said something to the men, they turned, and walked to an empty table. They sat and ordered from one of the saloon girls while Mayor Snow walked over to join Shaye at the bar.

"Sheriff, can I buy you another?" the mayor asked.

"Sure, why not."

Snow signaled the bartender for two beers.

"What's on your mind, Mayor?" Shaye asked, accepting the icy mug. "Who are your friends?"

Mayor Snow took a swig from his own mug and said, "Those are your two new deputies. Their names are Hawko and Tayback."

Shaye put his beer back down on the bar. He didn't know the men, but that didn't matter.

"What are you talkin' about?" Shaye asked. "I told you this mornin' —"

"Now, now, just hear me out," Snow said, putting his beer down and holding his hands out in a placating gesture. "They're good with their guns, and they'll take your orders."

"You think so?" Shaye asked.

The mayor looked at the two men, then

66

back at Shaye. "You saying you don't think they will?"

"I'm sayin' I've seen their type before," Shaye said. "They don't put their lives on the line for a deputy sheriff's pay."

Snow grabbed his beer, stared into it and took a sip.

"Oh, wait," Shaye said. "How much did you promise to pay them?"

"That doesn't matter."

"It does to me," Shaye said. "You think two money-guns are gonna take orders from a lawman who's bein' paid less than they are?"

Snow looked over at the two men again.

"So what do I do?" he asked. "I already told them they have the job."

Shaye once more picked up his beer.

"That was your mistake," he said. "Pay them off and send them on their way." He sipped from his mug. "Where did you find them, anyway?"

"They were just riding through town," he said. "Stopped for a while. When I saw them they were sitting in front of the hotel. I know the look too, Dan. I knew they were for hire."

"Well, not for this job," Shaye said. "I told you, I'm not puttin' a badge on a hired gun."

"I get it," the mayor said. "Pay them off, huh?"

"You have to."

"I don't suppose you'd consider —"

"Nope," Shaye said. "This is your mess to clean up. I already agreed to help you with Cole Doucette."

"Yeah, you did," the mayor confirmed. "Okay." He put his beer down and walked away.

Shaye watched the politician make his way over to the two gunmen, and decided to stay in the saloon during the exchange.

"We what?" Sam Hawko asked. He was the slightly older of the two.

"You don't have the job," the mayor said.

"But you said we did," Paul Tayback said. He was the larger of the men.

"I know I did," Snow said, "but I didn't check with the sheriff before I spoke."

"That's too bad," Hawko said. "We're still gonna need to get paid."

"Of course," Snow said. "For a . . . week?"

"Sure," Hawko said, "a week."

"It'll have to be fifty cents on the dollar, though," Snow added.

"What's that mean?" Tayback asked.

"Half," Hawko said. "He wants to pay us half."

"Oh, no," Tayback said.

"My partner's right," Hawko said. "We can't take half. He's a big boy. He eats a lot."

"Now look," Snow said, "I spoke out of turn and I can't, in good conscience, pay you in full for work you're not going to do."

"No fault of ours," Hawko said, shaking his head.

"You're right," Snow said, "the fault is mine, but I'm trying to be reasonable here."

"Reasonable would be to pay what you owe us," Hawko said.

"But I don't owe you anything because you didn't do a job," Snow said.

Hawko smiled at him. "Again, that's not our fault, Mayor. I think you better pay up."

Snow hesitated.

Tayback said, "Make up your mind, Mayor. You're a little low on law right now, so it ain't like you got other options."

At the mention of another option, Mayor Snow looked over at the bar to see if Shaye was still there.

THIRTEEN

Shaye saw the mayor look in his direction and set down his beer. He assumed the hired guns were giving the mayor a hard time as he tried to cancel their deal. As he shook his head and walked over to the three men, he wondered why Snow didn't just pay them.

"Problem here, Mr. Mayor?" he asked.

It wasn't the mayor who answered the question, but one of the other men.

"No problems, Sheriff," Sam Hawko said. "The mayor is just tryin' to go back on a deal we made."

"Look, fellas," Shaye said. "I'm the one who told the mayor it was no deal."

"That's okay, Sheriff," Hawko said. "If you don't want us, it's no problem. We just need to get paid."

"I told them I'd pay them half what I offered," the mayor said.

"That doesn't work for you men?" Shaye asked.

"Not at all," Hawko said. "We want what we're owed."

"Well," Shaye said, "seems to me you didn't do any work, so you're not owed anything."

"That's what the mayor's been tryin' to tell us," Hawko said. "And what we're sayin' is, that ain't our fault."

"I'm sorry," Mayor Snow said, "but I just can't pay the full amount."

"Well," Hawko said, "we ain't leavin' without our money."

"Now you're just bein' stubborn," Shaye said. "See, I think the mayor's offer of half was fair, but now I think you should just leave town."

Hawko studied Shaye for a few moments, then said, "If I'm right, Sheriff, you don't have any deputies to back your play."

"If I'm right . . . which one are you?"

"Hawko."

"If I'm right, Hawko," Shaye said, "I don't need any back-up."

The mayor took a few cautious steps back.

Hawko studied Shaye again, then frowned.

"Well," he said, "surely you'll let us stand first."

"Nope," Shaye said. "You want to skin

71

that hogleg, you're gonna have to do it from where you are."

Tayback looked at Hawko. No matter how fast a man was, he was at a disadvantage if seated, especially if seated at a table.

"Whataya say, boy?"

Hawko frowned.

"What're our options?" he asked.

"Draw or take your guns out slow, with two fingers, and put them on the table. Your choice."

"You'd make us walk outta here with no guns?"

"You can have them back," Shaye said, "unloaded."

"What if we just go out, load 'em up again, and come back in?"

"I think once you boys are outside the saloon," Shaye said, "you'll talk it over and come up with a better idea than that."

Hawko looked at Snow, then at Shaye again.

"The mayor didn't tell us your name," he said.

"It's Sheriff Dan Shaye," Mayor Snow said, before Shaye could speak up.

Hawko looked at Shaye, nodded, then looked at Tayback.

"Take out your gun, Paul."

"Yeah!" Tayback said like that was the only

move that made sense.

They removed their guns and gingerly laid them on the table.

"Now you can stand up and back away," Shaye said.

Both men did so.

"Mayor, unload both guns."

Mayor Snow stepped forward and, with shaky hands, ejected the shells from each weapon onto the table, then put the guns back down.

"Okay, boys," Shaye said, "take back your guns and walk on out."

"Sure, Sheriff," Hawko said. "We never meant you no disrespect."

"I know you didn't."

Hawko and Tayback picked up their empty guns and holstered them, then looked longingly at the bullets still rolling around on the table.

They started to walk to the doors, but Hawko turned to say one more thing.

"You know," he said to Shaye, "your mayor oughtta have more confidence in his lawman."

"I agree with you."

"Especially when it's Dan Shaye," Tayback said.

"Let's go, Paul," Hawko said.

Tayback actually touched the brim of his

hat and said, "Sheriff," conveying respect.

The saloon was so quiet that after the two men left, the sound of retreating horses could be easily heard. The two gunnies were riding out fast.

Shaye scooped up the bullets in his left hand, dropped them into the pocket of his vest, then looked at the mayor.

"Dan," Snow said, "I was just trying to help."

FOURTEEN

Thomas was frustrated.

He had ridden downstream two days ago, picked up the Fleming brothers' trail, and had been following it ever since.

Until two hours ago.

The terrain had become rock hard, and while he knew his father would be able to follow the trail anyway, Thomas had lost it. All he could do was continue to ride in the same direction and hope he could pick up the trail again.

He was riding in a desolate section of Arizona, south of Tucson, and just north of Mexico. They must have been heading for the border. If Thomas crossed into Mexico, he'd have to remove his badge and go on as a civilian. He didn't know if his father would approve of that, but he wouldn't find out about it until he got back to Vengeance Creek.

■ ■ ■ ■

An hour later, he was riding along the Santa Cruz River and came within sight of a town called Tubac. He had never been to Tubac, but he knew there was a history of Apache attacks there. In the early 'sixties, during the war, there was a siege between the male population, Confederate militia, and Apaches.

He also knew that after the siege, the town was deserted as its residents had left and gone to Tucson. There might still be some people living there, but it would be a very few.

He broke away from the river and headed for the town.

Red and Harry Fleming crossed the border into Mexico and headed for Nogales.

"That fuckin' town was a waste," Harry said. He was talking about Tubac.

"Hey," Red said, "we had somethin' to drink and somethin' to eat."

"Yeah, and you had a woman," Harry said. "Like we had time for that."

Red laughed.

"There's always time for a woman, brother," he said.

"With a posse on our trail?"

"You know," Red said, "I been thinkin' about that. If there was a posse after us, we woulda seen sign of them by now."

"What sign?"

"A bunch of riders would be kickin' up a dust cloud," Red said, "and we'd be seein' it."

"So you're sayin there's nobody after us?" Harry said, brightening.

"No, I ain't sayin' that," Red said. "A lawman like Dan Shaye ain't gonna let what we did go."

"So maybe he's trackin' us himself?"

"Or he sent his deputies."

Harry thought a moment. Then he brightened up again and said, "His sons."

"Right."

"Then all we gotta do is stop and wait for them," Harry said, "and bushwhack 'em. We can kill Shaye's sons."

"And why would we wanna do that, Harry?"

"They put me in a cell, Red," Harry said. "That older one, Thomas, I want him!"

"If we kill Shaye's sons, he'll never stop huntin' us," Red said.

"Hey," Harry said, "you're the fastest gun there is, Red. You could kill Thomas Shaye and Sheriff Shaye. No problem."

"Yeah, well," Red said, "we ain't gonna stop and wait for anybody. If they're gonna catch us, they'll hafta keep tryin'."

"And if they do catch up to us?"

Red turned his head and looked directly into his brother's eyes.

"Then we'll kill 'em," he said.

"Yes!" Harry Fleming said.

FIFTEEN

James followed the trail being left by Candy until it petered out after three days. He still had some water and a little beef jerky left, but he was going to need to stop somewhere for more supplies. He didn't have time to go hunting.

He decided to stop at the nearest town, outfit himself, and then set out again, hoping to pick up the trail. He'd hate to go back to Vengeance Creek and tell his father he'd lost Candy.

Or maybe he'd find out something in town.

Candy did everything Red Fleming had told him to do. He left a clear trail to allow a posse — or a single rider — to follow him for three days. At that point, he did everything he could to obliterate his trail, and then turned south. Red and Harry Fleming were heading for Mexico, and that was where Candy was going to meet them.

But first he had to get himself outfitted for the ride.

Flintlock was a small town three days' ride north of Vengeance Creek. James had never been there, but he knew his father had been there several times. Flintlock had its own town sheriff, but in Dan Shaye's opinion, the man wasn't much of a lawdog. They had a mercantile, though, a saloon, and a whore-house, so they were a good stopover for anybody who wanted to get outfitted, and maybe have a poke or two before going back on the trail.

He rode into town late in the afternoon. It seemed deserted except for a couple of men and a dog. The men were on opposite sides of the street and ignored him. Only the dog, who was standing right in the middle of the street, paid him any attention. One man was seated in a chair, whittling, while the other was seated in a chair, napping. That seemed a solid indication of what kind of town Flintlock was. The napping man's chair was leaning back against the front wall of the jail, so James wouldn't have been surprised if he was the sheriff.

James reined in his horse in front of the mercantile and dismounted. There were no other horses in sight as he wrapped his reins around a hitching post that leaned to one side.

He entered the store, found it small but well-stocked.

" 'Afternoon," an older man behind the counter greeted. "Can I help ya, Deputy?"

"Looks like you've got pretty much everything a man could need," James said.

"Oh, yeah," the man said, "there ain't much between here and Vengeance Creek. Lots of folks who can't make it there come here for their supplies. That's where yer from, ain't it? Vengeance Creek?"

"That's right," James said. "How did you know that?"

"Oh, lucky guess, is all," the man said. "Not too many lawmen come this way. Next town's about half a dozen miles east of here. What can I getcha?"

"Not much," James said. "I'm riding light. I need some jerky, coffee, water for my canteen."

"There's a waterin' hole 'bout a mile west of town, but I can help with that right here. Anythin' else? Ammunition maybe?"

"I'm pretty good in that area," James said. "Maybe a few cans of beans." James didn't want his saddlebags to be bulging with supplies. "And some bacon?"

"Comin' up."

"Oh," he said, "and I'll need a coffee pot and a frying pan." He figured he might as well have some hot coffee and food if he was going to be camping at night while he was trying to pick up Candy's trail again.

"How about a gunny sack to carry it in?" the man said. "Unless ya wanna pack yer saddlebags with a pot and pan. You can tie it to yer saddlehorn."

"That sounds like a good idea."

"I thought it might. I'll get these supplies ready fer ya right away."

"Much obliged."

James waited patiently while the man collected his items and brought them to the counter, then did his sums to come up with the final price.

"There ya go," the clerk said, handing James his handwritten bill. "I'm guessin' you'll need to turn that in when ya get back to town."

"I guess you're right."

James took out some money, paid his bill and tucked the piece of paper into his shirt pocket.

"This sounds like you've done all this before," James said, picking up his sack and supplies.

"Did," the man said, "lots of time. In fact,

82

just did it earlier this mornin'."

"You did?" James asked.

"Probably fer the man yer trackin'," he said. "You are trackin' a fella, ain'tcha?"

"I am, at that."

"Fella some older than you, kinda good-lookin', I guess, if yer a gal."

"That's him. What'd he buy?"

"Pretty much the same kinda stuff you just bought," the clerk said. "Seems he had a way to go."

"You know which direction?"

"South," the clerk said. "I snuck a look, since I figured he had law on his back trail."

"Did he say where he was going?"

"Naw, he didn't say much," the clerk said. "Pretty much just pointed. But he did go to the saloon before he left town. You should check there."

"Okay, I will," James said. "I'm much obliged, Mister . . ."

"Lennox," the man said, "Dave Lennox."

"I'm James Shaye."

"One of Dan Shaye's boys?"

"That's right."

Lennox stuck out his hand and said, "Glad to meetcha and glad to help. I saw your pa take the Travis boys in back in Hays, Kansas, in 'seventy-three."

"Did you know him?" James asked, shaking the man's hand.

"Naw, didn't meet 'im, but I seen what he did. Helluva lawman."

"Yes, he is," James said. "Uh, your lawman, is that him, sleeping in front of the jail?"

"That's him, all right."

"He didn't see my man, did he?"

"He never stirred from his chair," Lennox said. "He ain't moved for hours."

"I better get moving, then," James said. "I'll check the saloon. Thanks."

"Take care, Deputy."

There were three men in the saloon. One was the bartender. Another was slumped over the bar, while the third had his head down on a table.

"What can I getcha?" the bartender asked.

"Beer," James said. "If it's cold."

"It ain't."

"I'll take it, anyway."

"Comin' up."

James looked around at the other two men, the interior of the saloon. The tables and chairs seemed as wilted as the men.

"How many people you got in this town?" James asked as the bartender set his beer down.

"Not many," the man said. "Me and these

two, Dave Lennox over at the store, a few others, and some whores." James realized that the two men were the same two he'd seen on the street.

"What happened around here?" James asked. He sipped the beer, which was lukewarm, but wet.

The bartender shrugged. "Folks left. Me and Dave keep our places stocked for people who pass through, like you."

"And the fellow who came through this morning?"

"Yah, him, too," the man said. "Sometimes we get some cowhands, come to town to drink, use some whores, get some supplies and move on."

"That fellow this morning?" James asked. "Did he say where he was headed from here?"

The bartender looked at James's badge for the first time.

"You huntin' him?"

"I am."

"What'd he do?"

James stretched the truth.

"Broke a prisoner out of jail and killed a man."

The bartender shook his head.

"Naw, he didn't say where he was goin'," he said. "In fact, he didn't talk much at all, except to ask for a beer."

"That's pretty much what Lennox said." James put the beer down on the bar.

"Sorry I can't help ya."

"Yeah, me, too." He reached into his pocket for a coin.

"Beer's on the house, Deputy," the bartender said.

"Thanks."

James turned and walked out of the saloon, mounted his horse, and rode out of town, heading south.

Sixteen

Thomas rode into Tubac.

Nothing moved. There was not even a breeze. The main street was the most deserted thing he had ever seen in his life. It wasn't even midday yet, a time when most towns were busy.

It was a small town, so he was able to easily ride from one end to the other on the main street. Many of the buildings had broken or boarded-over windows and doors.

When he got to the end of the street he turned his horse and rode back. He'd followed what he thought were the tracks left by Red and Harry Fleming, but now he was seeing more than just two sets of hoof prints in the dirt. Perhaps the town wasn't as deserted as it appeared.

He reined in his horse in front of the small cantina and dismounted. That was when he smelled it. Something was cooking somewhere in town.

When he got to the batwing doors he stopped and took a deep breath. Sure enough, the odor of cooking food was coming from inside.

"Hello?" he called, without going through the doors.

He waited, and just when he was going to call out again, somebody came from out of the back room.

"Hola," she said.

She was an attractive Mexican woman in her thirties, wearing an apron and an off-the-shoulder peasant blouse.

"Do you speak English?" he asked.

"Si," she said, then, "yes, I do."

"Can I come in?"

"Of course," she said. "This is a cantina."

He pushed the batwing doors in and entered.

"I thought the town was deserted," he said.

"Almost," she told him. "Are you hungry?"

"Very."

"Please," she said, "sit. I will get you some food." She turned to head back to what was presumably the kitchen. "Do you have money?"

"I do."

She smiled happily and went into the

kitchen. Moments later she returned with two plates, one with meat and vegetables, and the other with tortillas.

"Would you like something to drink?" she asked. "Perhaps tequila?"

"Coffee would be fine, if my nose is working."

"I have a pot in the kitchen," she said.

Once again she disappeared, and this time returned with a pot and a cup.

"Thank you," he said again as she poured him a cup.

"Can I do anything else for you?"

"Yes," he said, "you could sit down with me while I eat. I'd like to ask some questions."

"I thought you might," she said, "when I first saw your badge." She walked to the bar, reached behind it for another cup, came back, sat and poured herself a cup of coffee. "I assume you're buying me a cup of coffee?"

"I am. What's your name?"

"Irma."

"My name's Thomas Shaye. You know," he said, "you look Mexican, but you don't sound it. And Irma's not a Mexican name."

"That's because I'm not," she said. "But this is a cantina, and this is what people expect me to look like."

"Do many people come here?" he asked.

"A few who live here," she said, "and those who pass through, like you."

"How many people live here?"

"Just a few," she said. "Those of us who are waiting for the town to come back to life."

"What about Apaches?"

"We ain't seen any Apaches here in years," she said. "The last major attack was 'sixty-one, and that's when people left."

"You were here then?"

She nodded. "I was a young girl. My parents didn't want to leave."

"Are they still here?"

She shook her head. "They both died and left me with this place."

"Why don't you leave?" he asked.

"Like I said," she replied. "We're waitin' for the town to come back to life. Meanwhile, this is all I got."

"You're a good cook," he told her.

"Uh-huh," she said. "That ain't all I'm good at. After you're finished eatin' we could go in the back." She ran her hand over her bare shoulder, tugged the blouse down a little further.

It was obvious what she was offering him.

"No," he said, "that's okay. I'm on the trail

90

of two men. Has anyone else been through here?"

"Yeah," she said, "earlier today."

"Did you feed them?" he asked.

"Yeah," she said, "and one of them did wanna go in the back."

"How long ago was that?"

"Hours."

"They say where they were goin' from here?"

"No," she said. "They didn't talk much."

"Did they talk to anybody else in town?"

"No," she said, "just me. I fed them, went in the back with one, then wrapped up some food for them to take with them."

"Which one went in the back with you?"

"The older one," she said.

"That was Red Fleming," he said. "The other one's his brother, Harry."

"Yeah," she said. "He called him Harry. Told him not to be so nervous."

"Harry was nervous?"

"Yeah. He didn't wanna go in the back with me, and he didn't want the other one to, either. The older one, he said, 'Take it easy, Harry. Have another drink while the lady entertains me.'" She laughed. "Ain't nobody called me a lady in a long time."

"That's too bad," he said. "Seems to me you are a lady."

91

She laughed again. "Seems to me if I was a lady I wouldn't be offerin' to go in the back with you."

"Everybody's gotta make a nickel." He realized he might have insulted her. "Not that I'm sayin' you're a nickel a poke."

"Don't worry," she said. "I'm way past havin' my virtue insulted."

"Well," he said, pushing his plate away, "you're still a helluva cook."

"You goin' after them?" she asked. "Right away?"

"I can't let them get too far ahead."

"You want me to pack some food for you? Won't take long."

"Sure, that'd be great. Thanks, Irma."

"I'll wrap up some enchiladas nice and tight," she promised, collecting the plates off the table.

He poured himself another cup of coffee, figuring there was no harm waiting a little longer for the food.

"Here you go, Deputy," she said, coming from the kitchen with some food wrapped in a napkin.

"Much obliged. Would you know how far we are from the Mexican border?"

"About twenty-five miles," she said. "They might be across it by now."

"I'll have to take that chance."

"You ain't gonna follow 'em, are ya?" she asked. "Your badge ain't no good over there."

"Maybe not," he said. "But my gun is. Thanks, Irma."

As he went out the doors she called out, "Stop in on your way back!"

She stepped outside as he rode away.

"Men!" she said.

SEVENTEEN

After five days, Dan Shaye started to worry about his boys. The badges on their chests would be no help to them if they crossed the border into Mexico. In fact, the tin would work against them if they ran into Mexican *bandidos* or *federales.*

Hopefully, the Fleming boys had gone off to the north, but they were already wanted in several states, so it was more likely they'd ride south. Now Thomas, he wouldn't hesitate to take the badge off, put it in his pocket, and follow them. James, on the other hand, while he might cross into Mexico, would probably keep the badge on. He was still inordinately proud of wearing it, kept it nice and shiny. If James rode into Mexico, he'd get into trouble sooner or later — unless he could find Thomas, first.

Shaye had taken to sitting in a chair in front of his office, watching the main street for Cole Doucette if and when he rode into town. Mayor Snow continued to insist he had word that Doucette was on his way.

"Last I heard," Snow had said the day before, "was that he was in Scottsdale. That only puts him a couple of days from here."

If that was true and Doucette was on his way to Vengeance Creek, he'd be there any time, now. But Shaye still wished he could have gone after the Fleming brothers with his sons. They were grown men, but they'd be doing a lot more growing up in Mexico.

Hawko and Tayback had not ridden far when they left Vengeance Creek. It was never their intention to actually go up against Sheriff Dan Shaye's gun. It was their job to check and see if he was there and what the situation was.

They had been in Scottsdale for two days after sending a telegram upon their arrival.

"How much longer are we gonna hafta wait?" Tayback complained.

"As long as it takes," Hawko said. "Those were our instructions."

"I never saw the instructions."

"They came with the money."

"As a matter of fact," Tayback said, "I never saw the money."

"Relax, Paul," Sam Hawko said. "We're gonna see plenty of money out of this.

Plenty of it."

They were sitting at a table in Miss Lottie's Saloon. Not the biggest watering hole in town, but the one they'd been instructed to patronize during their stay.

"I need a steak," Tayback said.

"That actually sounds good," Hawko said. "The steak house across the street?"

"Do we ever eat anywhere else?"

Hawko stood up. "Hey, the food's okay there."

Tayback stood and the two men walked to the batwing doors and stepped out onto the boardwalk. Across the street was the small steak house they'd been taking their meals at. Down the street from the hotel they'd been told to stay in. And, if they wanted female companionship, they had even been told which whorehouse to go to.

The Scottsdale streets were busy, and the two men waited for several wagons to go by before crossing over to the restaurant. But they didn't make it inside. After looking up and down the street, Hawko grabbed Tayback's arm.

"He's here!"

"Where?" Tayback looked around.

"Up the street," Hawko said, "ridin' in as bold as you please."

"Why not?" Tayback asked, seeing the

man now. "He's not wanted anywhere. After all, he's been released. He served his time."

"We'll wait here," Hawko said. "Doucette's gonna want a steak, too."

EIGHTEEN

James made a cold camp, not knowing how
close he might be to Dan Cannaday. He ate
some beef jerky and washed it down with
water from his canteen, then settled back to
consider his options.

After leaving Flintlock, he had ridden
south for the better part of a day before he
thought he had picked up the trail again.
Although he knew damned well he wasn't
the tracker his father, or even his brother,
were, he felt certain he recognized the tracks
left by Cannaday's horse.

His options were simple because he only
had one. There was no way he'd ever go
back to Vengeance Creek and admit to his
pa that he'd lost the trail. So he had no
choice but to keep going, no matter how
long it took. He only hoped his assumption
was right and that Cannaday was heading
south to meet up with the Flemings. That
way he'd be able to join up with Thomas,

and together they could take all three men in.

Meanwhile, he worried about what his pa might be going through back in town, especially if Cole Doucette showed up.

Only several miles ahead of James, Dan Cannaday made camp, building a small fire so he could make some coffee. He camped inside a circle of boulders so the fire couldn't be seen from a distance. He knew someone might smell the coffee, but he took the chance, although he decided not to do the same with a can of beans. And this while he was sure nobody was following him. If a posse had left Vengeance Creek, they were going to be after Red and Harry Fleming, not Candy. But there was no harm in being extra careful. He was less than a day's hard ride from Mexico. When he got there, he'd have plenty of warm food — and women.

Thomas rode into Nogales, Arizona, his badge secure in his shirt pocket. Right across the border was Nogales in the Mexican municipality of Sonora. He was going to ride there eventually, so he didn't want anyone on this side of the border to see his badge, in case he ran into them on the other side.

Nogales — both of them — being border towns, were very busy. There were other riders and wagons moving down the street alongside of him, so he was drawing no special attention — especially not with his badge hidden. He rode directly to the sheriff's office and dismounted. After tying off his horse, he mounted the boardwalk and entered.

Three men were in the office, one wearing the sheriff's badge, the other two with their backs to Thomas. The conversation going on was not a friendly one. He hadn't heard the words, but the voices were raised until he walked in. Then they all stopped and looked at him.

"Am I interrupting somethin'?" Thomas asked.

"Who are you?" one of the men demanded. He was an older fellow, wearing trail clothes.

"Relax, Jason," the sheriff said. "This is my office, remember?" The man with the badge looked at Thomas, who thought he had very tired eyes for a man in his thirties. "Can I help you?"

"I don't wanna interrupt, Sheriff," Thomas said. "I can come back."

"No, that's okay," the sheriff said. "These men were just leavin'."

"Sheriff, we ain't done —" the other man said.

"We're done for now, Mr. Gentry. I've got work to do."

"Come on, Dave," Jason said. "We'll come back later. Maybe the sheriff will be more cooperative."

The two men gave Thomas a look, walked to the door and left.

"That's just somethin' you have to deal with in this job," the sheriff said.

Thomas took his badge out and showed it to the man.

"Deputy Sheriff, Vengeance Creek," the sheriff read. "So, you know."

"Oh, yes," Thomas said. "My father's been a lawman for thirty years. My brother and me, we're his deputies now, and we know what you have to deal with in a town."

"Wait a minute," the lawman said. "Are you talkin' about Dan Shaye?"

"That's right," Thomas said. "My dad. I'm Thomas Shaye."

"Well, this is a great pleasure," the sheriff said, extending his hand. "My name's Frank Dewey. I've never met your dad, but I've heard of him, and I'd heard he took the job in Vengeance Creek with his sons, you and . . ."

". . . my younger brother, James."

101

"Right, right. Hey, have a seat. You want a cup of bad coffee?"

"Is there any other kind in a jailhouse?" Thomas asked. "Sure."

Thomas sat while Dewey went to a pot-belly stove in the corner, poured two cups, handed one to Thomas and then sat behind his desk, holding the other.

"So what can I do for you, Deputy?"

"I'm passin' through your town on my way to Nogales, in Sonora," Thomas said. "I'm trackin' the Fleming brothers, Red and Harry."

"I've heard of Red Fleming," Dewey said. "He's deadly. I never heard of his brother."

"Well, Harry thinks he's Red," Thomas sad. "He gunned down a man in Vengeance Creek and I tossed him in a cell. We were waitin' for a judge, when his brother came to town, broke him out and killed another man."

"So are you riding in advance of a posse?"

"No, I'm trackin' them alone," Thomas said. "My father sent my brother on another assignment, but he couldn't leave the town unprotected." He didn't bother telling Sheriff Dewey about the possibility that Cole Doucette might come to Vengeance Creek with bad intentions on his mind.

"So you tracked them here?"

102

"I tracked them as far as I could before I lost the trail," Thomas admitted. "But they were headed this way. I'm thinkin' they're headed for Mexico. They're wanted in enough places that Mexico would be a good idea."

"And are you plannin' to follow them across the border?" Dewey asked. "With your badge in your pocket?"

Thomas put the tin back in his pocket and said, "It ain't gonna do me much good over there."

"That's for sure," Dewey said. "You ain't gonna have no jurisdiction there."

"I know that," Thomas said, "but one of the men who was killed was a friend of mine."

"So it's personal."

"It's both," Thomas said. "Harry was my prisoner. It's my duty to bring him back."

"What can I do?"

"Well, I was gonna ask if you'd seen the Flemings in your town," Thomas said, "but I'm guessin' the answer's no."

"Sorry, Deputy," Dewey said, "but I ain't seen hide nor hair."

"Do you mind if I ask around town a bit?" Thomas asked. "I'll only be here long enough to get somethin' to eat and have a beer."

"Ask away," Dewey said, "and if there's anythin' I can do, let me know."

"I will." Thomas sipped the coffee, then set the cup down on the desk and stood up. "You were right. That coffee is awful."

NINETEEN

In Nogales, Mexico, Red Fleming stuffed his face full of enchiladas, tacos and rice while his brother watched him, nursing a glass of tequila.

"I don't know how you can eat," Harry Fleming said.

"Relax," Red said. "Ain't we talked about this already? We're in Mexico. Even if Shaye or his boys come after us, they got no . . . what's it called . . . authority down here. We can kill them and nobody's gonna care."

"As long as they ain't comin' with a full posse."

Red pointed at Harry with the taco in his hand.

"If they took the time to put together a posse, then they're even farther behind us. You should have somethin' to eat and keep up your strength."

Harry eyed the food in the middle of the table, then put down his glass and piled some food on his plate.

"Attaboy, Harry," Red said. "Eat up! Then we'll find us some fine Mexican whores!"

Harry looked over at the bar, where two girls were watching them eat. One of them had served their food, showing them her bare shoulders while she did it. Maybe Red was right. Maybe he should relax.

Across the border, in Nogales, Arizona, Thomas indulged himself with a steak dinner and a hotel room, and put his horse up in the livery for some feed and a night's rest. In the morning he'd cross the border into Sonora.

While he ate, he described the Fleming brothers to the waiter, asked if he'd seen two such men. The waiter shook his head and asked Thomas if he wanted more bread.

In the saloon across from the steak house, Thomas asked the bartender if he'd seen the Fleming brothers.

"Don't know 'em," the man said.

Thomas described them.

"Ain't seen 'em. You want another beer?"

He talked to a couple of the saloon girls, asked the same questions.

"Don't know why you're lookin' for two men, handsome," one girl said to him. She was a blonde, in her twenties, and very pretty. "Why don't we go upstairs for a while?"

"I would do that, honey, but I'm afraid you'd be too much of a distraction, and I've got things to do."

"Well, come see me if you change your mind." She sashayed away.

The other woman was about ten years older than the first, with black hair and a face that had been pretty once, but she'd been doing this job too long for it to stay that way. Now she was attractive, but brittle looking at the same time. Her body had become a little thick in the waist, and her breasts threatened to spill out of the top of her dress. She was less flirty after he asked his question.

"Why you lookin' for them?" she asked. "Messin' with that kind is just gonna get you killed."

"So you've seen them?"

"Ain't seen 'em," she said, "but I heard of 'em. Well, Red Fleming, anyway. He's a killer."

"That he is," Thomas said, "and that's why I'm lookin' for him. Why don't you let me buy you a drink?"

"Upstairs?" she asked.

"Down here's good enough."

"Drinks are cheaper upstairs, honey," she

told him.

"That's okay," he said. "I'll pay."

"Suit yourself. Hey, Al!" she called the bartender. "Gimme a drink. The cowboy here's payin'. And give him another beer."

They took their drinks to a table, and had their pick since the saloon was only about half full. The blonde girl saw Thomas sitting with the woman and frowned.

"What's your name?"

"Belle."

"So, tell me about Red Fleming, Belle," Thomas said.

"Oh, like I said," she went on, "I don't know him, I just know of him. I'd hate to see a sweet boy like you end up dead because you didn't know what you were gettin' into."

"Believe me," Thomas said, "I know." He took his badge out of his pocket and showed it to her. "I'm trackin' both brothers, and aim to bring 'em in for murder."

"Well," she said, sitting back, "a deputy. I'm impressed. Guess I had you figured for a cowboy."

"You figured wrong," Thomas said, putting the badge back in his pocket.

"Why ain't you wearin' it?"

"Because I'm goin' into Mexico tomorrow," he said. "That's where I figure the

Fleming boys are, unless you tell me I'm wrong."

"There's no way I can tell you that, Deputy," she said. "But why don't you spend the night with me? At least you'll have that to think about when Red Fleming is killin' you."

"I think I'll pass, thanks." He finished his beer and stood up. "Thanks for the offer, though. And the advice."

"I just wish I'd been able to help you," she said.

"Don't worry about it," he said. "I think you did."

TWENTY

Thomas took up a position across the street from the saloon after dark, and waited. Something about what Belle had told him didn't ring true. His father had told both him and James, long ago, to trust their instincts. If something didn't sound true, it probably wasn't.

So he decided to see if Belle went someplace in town that he might find interesting. Maybe the Flemings were there, and she was covering for them. Maybe everybody — including the sheriff — was covering for them because it was Nogales.

He'd wait and see.

It was more than an hour before Belle finally came out the batwing doors. The saloon was busier than it was when he'd been inside. And there she was, still wearing her dress, but covering her shoulders and breasts with a shawl. She came out the doors, turned right and started walking at a brisk pace.

Remaining on his side of the street, he followed.

At this time of night, in a cafe that busy, a saloon girl should have been at work. The fact that she was outside and rushing like that had to mean something. He just hoped she wasn't checking on a sick friend or mother.

Keeping her in sight wasn't hard. His eyes were used to the shadows, and the streets of Nogales were empty this time of night. It didn't take long to find out she wasn't going to see her mother. After three blocks, she turned right and went down a dark side street. Thomas hurriedly crossed and followed her.

On the main street there was occasional light from the odd street lamp or coming from a window, but on this street there didn't seem to be any. However, Belle knew exactly where she was going and moved at a fast, surefooted pace.

Thomas, trying to keep up and not lose sight of her, barely avoided a couple of bad spills as he skirted the odd barrel or box that blocked the boardwalk for some reason.

Finally she left the street and cut down between buildings. He stopped at the mouth of the alley to watch and listen. It was pitch dark down there and he couldn't see her at all. Suddenly he heard a knocking, and then a door opened, bathing both Belle and the alley in bright light. Whoever had opened the door for her stepped back and she entered. The door closed behind her, once again leaving the alley in darkness.

Thomas entered and moved slowly toward where he thought the door was. As he crept along in the darkness, he noticed there were windows, but they were blocked from inside so that no light came out.

He felt along the wall and found the door as his eyes finally adjusted to the pitch black. Looking down, he saw no light from beneath it. Either the room just inside was dark, or someone had blocked the crack beneath the door, as they had blocked the windows.

He listened at the door, didn't hear anything. Next he tried the door knob, but the door was locked. He figured there was only one way he was going to get inside.

He knocked.

Inside, two men were listening to Belle tell them about Thomas, "the deputy."

"He wanted to know about Red," she said.

"What did you tell him?" Adam Grey asked.

"Nothin'," she said. "I told him I didn't know Red Fleming, only heard of him."

"Did he believe you?" Johnny Widmark asked.

"Sure he did."

Widmark looked up from his seated position near the older Grey, who was standing.

"Sure he did," he said. "He musta."

"We'll have to get word across the border to Red," Grey said. "He'll wanna know."

"He already knows," Widmark said. "He told us, remember?"

"He said somebody might come after him, he didn't know who," Grey said. "Probably a badge. We'll have to tell him who it is."

"We don't know who it is," Widmark said. "Just a deputy."

"We'll find out," Widmark said.

"How?" Belle asked.

"We'll ask the right person."

"And who's that?" Widmark asked.

"Who do ya think?"

"The sheriff?"

"Got it the first time," Grey said. "Is he in the other room?"

"Yeah," Widmark said. "He's bettin' on the fights."

"Okay."

"So what do I do?" Belle asked.

"Just go back to work," Grey said. "And don't —"

At that moment there was a knock at the alley door.

"Who's that?" Belle asked.

"Relax, it's probably somebody lookin' for a game," Widmark said.

"Should I get it?" Grey asked.

"I'll get it," Widmark said. "Just in case. You take Belle out the front."

"Adam —" Belle said.

"Go ahead!" he said.

"Come on!" Widmark snapped, grabbing her arm. He pulled her into the game room.

Widmark walked into the adjoining room, to the alley door, and opened it.

TWENTY-ONE

"I'm lost," was the first thing Thomas could think to say when the door was opened by a man wearing a gambler's three-piece suit.

"Are you?"

"It's kind of dark out here."

"So it is," Grey said. "Come on in."

Thomas entered, found himself in what looked like a storage room only partially lit by the light coming in the door from another room.

"My name's Adam Grey. This way, please," Grey said, leading Thomas through that door.

Here he saw a small room with four chairs and a burning lamp on a table.

"Are you here for a game?" Grey asked.

"A game?" Thomas asked. "I don't know what you mean."

"Why are you here then, sir? And who are you?"

"My name is Thomas Shaye," he said, taking out his badge. "I'm a deputy sheriff from Vengeance Creek."

"Vengeance Creek?" the man repeated. "You're a little off your patch, aren't you, Deputy?"

"I'm trackin' two killers."

"And you tracked them to the door of my establishment?"

Thomas looked around curiously.

"Just what kind of establishment is this?" he asked.

"I provide . . . games, for people to bet on."

"A gambling hall?"

"You could say that," the man said, "but I don't supply the usual games. You won't find poker and faro. The town has certain limitations on those games."

"So your games are illegal?"

"You could say that."

"Does the sheriff know about this?"

"You could ask him," Grey said. "He's in the next room."

Thomas frowned. He didn't like crooked lawmen, but that wasn't what he was in Nogales for.

"Never mind," Thomas said. "I was followin' a woman and she came here."

"A woman? Does she have a name?"

"Belle," Thomas said. "That's all I know.

116

She works in a saloon —"

"I know who Belle is, Deputy," Grey said. "She was here, but isn't anymore."

"Where is she?"

"You might find her back at the saloon."

Thomas deliberated a moment, then said, "I assume she came here to tell you I'm lookin' for Red Fleming."

"Red Fleming?" Grey asked, appearing surprised. "Is that who you're tracking? He's a killer."

"That's what I said," Thomas replied. "He killed a man in Vengeance Creek, and so did his brother."

"The same man?"

Thomas grew impatient.

"Does that matter?" he demanded.

Grey put his hand up and said, "I was just asking for clarification."

"They each killed a man," Thomas said, "and I'm gonna bring them back to stand trial."

"Not to hang?"

"That'll be up to the judge."

"So you intend to bring these men back alive?"

"That'll be up to them."

"And you think you can do that?" Grey asked. "Bring in both of the Fleming boys?"

"It's my job," Thomas said. "Don't matter

if I think I can do it or not."

"That's very . . . noble of you, Deputy. Say, I've got an idea."

"What?"

"I don't know these fellows, of course, but there are plenty of men in the other room who would like to bet on whether or not you can bring them in. What do you say? I'll cut you in for a piece of the action."

"And if I get killed?"

"I'll pay double. See, I'm going to back you."

"So that's the kind of games you run?" Thomas asked. "Where a man's life is the stake?"

Grey shrugged his shoulders. "It makes things interesting."

"And how does the sheriff feel about that?"

"Why don't you ask him?" Grey asked. "Like I said, he's in the other room. But you better wait until after the fight."

Thomas compressed his lips and bit his tongue. He had his father's impatience for lawmen with even a hint of dishonesty. It didn't matter if they were taking money to look the other way, or for shooting strays, none of it sat right with the Shaye men.

"If you send a message to Red Fleming," Thomas said to Grey, "tell him I'm comin'

118

for him."

"I told you, I don't —"

"Yeah, yeah," Thomas said, cutting him off, "you don't know him. Just give him the message."

Thomas turned to head for the alley door.

"Deputy?"

He turned.

"You can use the front door, if you want."

"The alley way will do fine," Thomas said, and left.

TWENTY-TWO

Thomas awoke the next morning feeling wholly dissatisfied with his stop in Nogales. If anything, all he'd succeeded in doing was letting Red Fleming know he was behind him, and alone. Comfortable with the fact that there wasn't an entire posse on their trail, the Fleming brothers might just turn and fight — or, more likely, bushwhack him.

As a U.S. lawman — and local, to boot, not federal — he would be perfectly justified in turning around and riding back to Vengeance Creek. He wasn't even concerned about what his father and brother would think, because he'd be more disappointed in himself. There was no way he was going to allow the Mexican border to keep him from bringing two killers to justice. He'd keep the badge in his pocket, and when he dragged the Flemings back into the U.S., he'd take it out and pin it back on.

He checked out of his hotel and walked to a café he'd found halfway between the hotel and the livery for his breakfast. He was enjoying his ham and eggs when the sheriff walked in and came over to his table.

"Mind if I sit?"

"Go ahead," Thomas said. "Want some food?"

"I had breakfast, thanks."

"How about some coffee?"

"That I'll always say yes to," the local lawman said, "as long as it ain't mine."

The sheriff sat, righted a cup on the table and poured himself a cup while Thomas continued to eat.

"What's on your mind this mornin', Sheriff?" Thomas asked.

"You are," Sheriff Dewey said. "I heard you talked with Adam Grey last night."

"I did."

"Well, whatever he told you," Dewey said, "I'd take with a grain of salt."

"I figured out that much for myself," Thomas said around a piece of ham. "What've you got for me that I don't already know?"

"Okay," the lawman said, "I know you don't think much of me. I've got a gambling problem —"

"Hey," Thomas said, cutting him off,

121

"that's between you and whatever you believe in. I ain't here to judge you, but I don't like bein' lied to. You told me you didn't know Red Fleming."

"And I don't," Dewey said. "That wasn't a lie. But Grey, he knows every outlaw and thief who rides through here. They have to pay him some kind of tribute. So he knows Fleming, and he probably knows where he is. I came to warn you. Red Fleming probably knows you're comin'."

Thomas ate the last of his eggs, then sat back in his chair.

"I know that, too," he said.

"Well then, maybe you don't know this," Dewey said. "They're still in Nogales, right across the border."

Thomas sat forward.

"You're right, I didn't know that," he said. "Not for sure, anyway."

"Well, good." Dewey finished his coffee and stood up. "Then maybe I helped you."

"You can help me more by ridin' over there with me," Thomas said.

"Now that I can't do, Deputy," Dewey said. "You know that. No jurisdiction."

"Is there any law over there?"

"Yeah," Dewey said, "their own kind of law."

"Okay then," Thomas said. "Thanks."

122

"You headin' out now?" Dewey asked.

"Not sure," Thomas said. "I'm gonna have another cup of coffee and consider my options."

"Fair enough," Dewey said. "Watch your back."

"I will," Thomas said.

The sheriff walked out, and Thomas waved the waiter over so he could pay his bill and get to the livery before Dewey decided to go and talk to Adam Grey.

TWENTY-THREE

Across the border, Red and Harry Fleming were eating breakfast.

"What do they call these again?" Harry asked.

"Huevos rancheros," Red said. "Jesus, Harry, if we're gonna be down here a while you're gonna hafta learn some Spanish."

"And these are what?" Harry asked, looking at what was on his fork.

"They're eggs!"

"Ain't no eggs like I ever seen," Harry complained.

"Just put 'em in a tortilla and eat 'em," Red said. "I like 'em just fine."

Harry did as his brother said, loaded some of the dubious-looking eggs into a tortilla, rolled it up and bit into it.

"So, how long we gonna be down here, again?"

"At least until Candy gets here," Red said, "maybe longer."

"Why we gotta wait for him?"

"Because Candy's been ridin' with me a long time," Red said, "and he'll have some information for us."

"Like wha—"

"Oh, just shut up and eat, Harry!" Red snapped. "If you hadn't gone to that town to get your ashes hauled, we wouldn't be in this mess right now."

"I told you that guy deserved killin'!"

"I don't care! Just eat and shut up."

Morosely, Harry bit into his tortilla, wishing he had some bacon.

Later, while Red was in his room with the waitress, Harry Fleming took a walk around town. Nogales was a poor excuse for a town, not a place Harry wanted to spend a lot of time in. But Red liked the food, and he had a woman, and he wasn't worried about a posse crossing the border. Harry thought about moving along on his own, but the last time he'd done that, he'd gotten into trouble in Vengeance Creek.

He went into a general store, looked at some *sombreros* and *serapes,* bought himself a licorice stick and went outside. Just as he stepped out the door, he saw a rider, one he recognized, and ducked back inside.

Damn it!

He waited for the man to move on so he could step out again. He hit the street running, heading for the hotel. When he got there, he ran right to his brother's door and burst in.

Red was pulling on his trousers and stopped to stare at his brother

"You just missed her," he said. "Mighta got a look at her naked."

"He's here," Harry said, "just rode in."

"Who?"

"The deputy," Harry said. "The one who arrested me. Thomas Shaye."

Red straightened up.

"Is he alone?"

"He was when I saw him."

"What was he doin'?"

"Just ridin' in."

"So he just got here," Red said, grabbing his shirt and pulling it on.

"What are we gonna do?"

"We're gonna make sure he's alone before we do anythin'," Red said.

"And then we'll kill 'im?"

"We'll see, Harry," Red said. "Don't be in such a hurry to kill a lawman."

"We're in Mexico, Red," Harry said. "He ain't no lawman here."

"That's true," Red said, strapping on his gunbelt. "That's very true."

"So we're gonna do it, then?"

"If we do it, Harry," Red said, "we'll do it when I say so. Understand?"

"Yeah, yeah . . ."

"After all," Red went on, "he's here because you went off by yourself and got into trouble."

"I get it, Red," Harry said. "I get it!"

"Okay, then," Red said, "let's find out if Deputy Shaye is here alone."

Thomas Shaye rode into Nogales on the Mexican side of the border, badge in his pocket, eyes peeled for any sign of Red or Harry Fleming. It wouldn't do for either one to see him before he saw them. But he was prepared for anything. If they ran into each other on the street, he had no qualms about drawing his gun.

Nogales on the Mexican side was quite different from Nogales on the U.S. side. For one thing, it seemed dirtier, dustier, and the buildings all looked as if they would fall over in a stiff breeze. He reined in his horse in front of the Cantina Rosita and dismounted. Inside the place was practically empty, with a couple of men dozing beneath their tilted *sombreros.* He walked to the bar and uttered the only word of Spanish he knew.

"Cerveza."

"Si, señor."

The squat Mexican bartender set a mug of beer in front of him. He took two sips, knowing it wasn't going to be cold. But at least it was wet.

"Thanks."

"Por nada."

He turned with the mug in his hand and looked over the interior of the place. He and the bartender were the only men who were awake. The five others seated at tables — three alone, two together — were all dozing over their drinks. And from the looks of them, they were all Mexicans.

He turned back to the bar.

"Any *gringos* in town?" he asked.

"Si, señor."

"Where?"

The bartender pointed at Thomas, who laughed.

"Okay, what about other than me?"

"Perhaps a few," the bartender said, with a shrug. "Here and there."

"Nobody . . . noticeable?"

"Señor?"

"You know," Thomas said, "recognizable? Wanted names?"

"No one like that, *señor,*" the man said. "Not that I know of."

"I see." Thomas paid for his beer.

128

"Where's the nearest livery stable?"

"At the end of the street, *señor.*"

"Thanks."

"Señor," the bartender said, "you are a bounty hunter?"

"No," Thomas said, "I'm not," and left the cantina.

TWENTY-FOUR

Red Fleming told Harry to remain in his hotel room until he came back.

"Why?"

"Because Shaye knows you, dummy," Red said. "If he sees you, he'll know we're here. Just lie low until I come back."

"Don't you kill 'im without me," Harry warned his brother.

"I ain't goin' near him," Red said. "I just wanna find out if he's alone."

Red left his unhappy brother sitting on his bed, and departed from the hotel.

Naturally, he didn't know where Thomas Shaye had gone. Most likely he got a drink, or went to a hotel, or stopped at the sheriff's office. Red decided to have a drink first, and went to the biggest cantina in town. He was lucky. As he started to approach the front door opened and Shaye stepped out. Red quickly jumped back up onto the

boardwalk across the street, and into a doorway.

Shaye picked up his horse's reins and
started walking down the street, probably to
the nearby livery stable.

Red Fleming gave him a little bit of a head
start, then followed.

Thomas found the livery but had to wake
the hostler up to make arrangements for his
horse.

"Sorry, *señor*," the man said, "but it is
siesta time."

"Then I'm sorry, but my horse needs
tendin' to."

The hostler yawned and said, "Of course,
señor. And how long will you be stayin'?"

"I don't know," Thomas said. "I guess that
depends on how long it takes me to find
what I'm lookin' for."

Most men might have asked him what he
was looking for, but the fiftyish hostler was
probably more concerned with getting back
to his *siesta,* so he only nodded and took
Thomas's horse to a stall after the deputy
had removed his saddlebags and rifle.

Thomas left the livery. On the way there,
he had passed both a hotel and the sheriff's
office. He decided to first go to see the
sheriff. He found the office, but did not

knock on the door for fear of it collapsing beneath his fist. Instead he simply opened it and entered.

The interior seemed both fusty and dirty, as did the man behind the desk who, at that moment, was leaning back in his chair with his feet up, dozing. His chair was balanced only on its rear legs.

Thomas knew he was going to have to interrupt another *siesta*.

He cleared his throat, but the man at the desk didn't stir. He got closer and saw the sheriff's badge on the man's shirt, as opposed to a deputy's badge. He cleared his throat again, and this time the man moved, but didn't wake. He waved a hand in front of him, as if warding off a fly.

"Sheriff!" Thomas yelled.

The sheriff's feet immediately came down off his desk, and his chair came down with a bang onto its front legs.

He opened his eyes and blearily tried to focus on Thomas.

"Señor?"

"Sorry to disturb you, Sheriff," Thomas said.

"No, no," the man said, waving Thomas's apology off, "what can I do for you, *señor?*"

He was a fairly young man, although probably ten years or so older than Thomas.

"My name is Thomas Shaye," Thomas said, digging his badge out of his shirt pocket. "I'm a deputy from Vengeance Creek, Arizona."

"Arizona," the sheriff said. "I am afraid you have no authority here, Deputy."

"I understand that," Thomas said, tucking the badge away again, "but I'm pursuin' two men who murdered a friend of mine. That's why my badge is in my pocket."

"Well," the man said, "as you can see, my badge is on my chest. I am Sheriff Alfonso Perez Montoya. Who are these men you are looking for, Deputy?"

"The Fleming brothers," Thomas said. "Red and Harry. We had Harry in our jail for murder, and Red broke him out. In doin' so they killed a guard."

"That is sad, *señor,* very sad," Sheriff Montoya said. "You said 'we,' *señor?*"

"My father's the sheriff back in Vengeance Creek," Thomas said, "Daniel Shaye. My brother, James, is the other deputy."

"Ah," Montoya said, his eyes lighting up, "I have heard of this Sheriff Daniel Shaye. He is *muy malo,* is he not? A very bad man to cross?"

"Very bad," Thomas said.

"And you, *señor,* you take after your *padre?*"

133

"I do," Thomas said.

"So you are *muy malo*?"

"I'm *malo* enough to do my job, Sheriff Montoya."

"But again, *señor,* you are not here doing your job, *es verdad*? This is a personal matter for you."

"It's personal," Thomas said, "but I plan to take them back to Vengeance Creek for trial."

"Ah, then you do not intend to kill them," Sheriff Montoya said. "You will forgive me, but the way you wear your gun . . . you strike me as a man who settles his business with *la pistola* — your gun."

"On occasion," Thomas admitted.

"But not on this occasion, eh?"

"I hope not," Thomas said. "That's likely gonna be up to them."

"Well," Montoya said, "I must tell you I have not seen these men in my town."

"They'd probably have been here in the past few days," Thomas said.

"To tell you the truth," Montoya went on, "I have not even heard of these men, so I would not know them if I saw them." He shrugged. "Perhaps they were here, passing through."

"And kept a low profile, you mean."

"*Si,*" Montoya said, slapping his palm on

his desk, "that is what I mean, a low profile. If they were even here."

"I see," Thomas said. "Well, I just wanted to check in with you, let you know I was here, as a courtesy."

"I appreciate that, *señor.*"

"I'm gonna check into a hotel," Thomas continued, "take a quick look around your town, and then I'll probably leave in the mornin'."

"That would be wise, *señor,*" Montoya said. "They are probably just ahead of you."

"Probably."

"The hotel above the Cantina Rosita is very fine, *señor,*" the sheriff said, with a smile. "You will like your room very much."

"Ah, I just came from there," Thomas said. "Didn't realize they had rooms."

"Oh, *si, señor,*" Montoya said, "very fine rooms, and good food. And, if you like, very pretty *señoritas.*" Montoya kissed his finger-tips. *"Muy bonita."*

"Well," Thomas admitted, "I like pretty girls. And good food."

"Si, señor," Montoya said, with a laugh, "we all like the pretty girls."

"Thank you for your time, Sheriff."

"Por nada, señor, por nada," Montoya said, expansively. "Enjoy your time in Nogales."

"I'll sure try," Thomas said, and left.

He stopped just outside the door, looked up and down the street. The sheriff had obviously been lying about one thing. Any lawman in an area near Arizona, Nevada, New Mexico, or Old Mexico — would have heard of the Fleming Brothers. To claim that he had never heard of them put everything else he had said in doubt.

Even the information about the Cantina Rosita — but Thomas would quickly find out about that himself.

TWENTY-FIVE

Red Fleming watched Thomas Shaye come out of the sheriff's office. He recognized him from Vengeance Creek. Red backed into a doorway as Shaye looked both ways on the street. Then when the deputy started walking, he followed from a safe distance all the way to the saloon, where he took up a position across the street in an alley.

Thomas went to the Cantina Rosita, and the bartender greeted him in a friendly manner.

"*Señor,* you are back!" he said happily.

"I was told I could get a room and a meal here," Thomas said. He didn't say anything about a pretty *señorita.*

"But of course, *señor,*" the bartender said. "We have very fine rooms upstairs."

"And you have one available right now?"

"*Si,*" the man said. He reached under the bar and came out with a key. "Number two, just for you."

Thomas accepted the key. "I'd like to put my things in the room, and then come down and eat somethin'."

"*Si, señor,*" the bartender said. "We do a very fine supper."

"That'll do," Thomas said. "I'll be right down."

Thomas went up to his room, which he found to be almost as small as one of the jail cells back in the Shayes' jail. The mattress was paper thin, the flimsy dresser was covered with dust, as was the window sill. The window overlooked the street. He peered out for several moments, looking down at the *siesta*-time front street. He was about to turn away when he spotted something else, something odd.

Red Fleming saw Thomas Shaye in the window of a room above the Cantina Rosita, and quickly stepped back into the alley to avoid being seen. If the deputy saw him and came out to challenge him, he might end up being in a shootout in the street, and he wasn't ready for that. He'd heard some stories about Shaye's speed with a gun. Red was a gang leader, a planner, and a leader of men. Although he was fast with a gun, it was not something that was at the top of his own list of accomplishments. Facing Thomas Shaye out in the street was in his future plans, but only when he was ready. That kind of foolishness was his brother, Harry's, idea of a plan. But Red knew when they did challenge the deputy, it would be the two of them together, or himself alone. He'd not let Harry ever meet Shaye by himself.

He peered around the building from the alley and saw that Shaye's window was empty. He decided to get closer.

Thomas backed away from the window.

There was a man across the street in an alley, watching the building. It was either one of the Fleming brothers, or the sheriff had put somebody on his tail. He decided to see to his personal needs before anything. That meant a wash, a drink, and a meal.

Red Fleming peered into the cantina, didn't see Shaye anywhere. There were only a few people inside, and the bartender. He moved to one of the front windows, which was covered with grime, but still afforded him a view of the inside. He settled down to watch and determine whether or not Thomas Shaye was alone in Nogales.

■ ■ ■ ■

Thomas came down and saw one of the cantina tables set for a meal.

"Here you go, *señor,*" the bartender said, coming over to stand next to the table. "A fine meal."

"It looks good," Thomas said. "Thanks."

"*Cerveza* with the food?"

"Yes, please."

Thomas sat down at the table, which was covered with platters of meat, beans, vegetables, and tortillas. He spread one of the tortillas on a plate, shoveled food onto it, then rolled it up and took a bite.

"How is it, *señor?*" the bartender asked, returning with the beer.

"It's very good," Thomas said. "Thank you for this and the beer." He looked around. "When does this place liven up?"

"Right after *siesta* time," the bartender said. "Customers will begin coming in to drink and eat and . . ."

"And?"

"And see my girls."

"The pretty *señoritas,*" Thomas said.

"*Si,*" the bartender said.

"What's your name?"

"I am Manolito, *señor,*" the man said.

"Everyone calls me Mano."

"Well, Mano," Thomas said, "I'm still lookin' for two men, brothers, who robbed a bank in my town, Vengeance Creek."

"Like I told you, *señor*," Mano said, "I have not seen any such men here in Nogales."

"Maybe they just haven't come into your place," Thomas said. "How many other hotels are there in town? And cantinas?"

"There are three hotels," Mano said, "and many cantinas. I can tell you where they all are. Maybe you will find the men you are looking for at one of them."

Thomas continued to eat and listened while Mano gave him the lineup of hotels and cantinas.

"You're bein' very helpful, Mano," he said, then. "Why is that?"

"*Señor*," the bartender said, reproachfully, "I am a law-abiding citizen of Mexico."

"Uh-huh," Thomas said, taking that comment with a full grain of salt. "And?"

"And perhaps," the bartender said with a shrug of his shoulders, "when you catch the men you are looking for, if there is a reward . . ."

"I see," Thomas said, rubbing his jaw. "Well, I'm sure they're wanted somewhere. And if your information helps me catch them, I don't see any reason why you shouldn't get the reward money."

"*Señor,*" the barman said, with a very broad smile, "you have made me a very happy man. I will leave you now to enjoy your meal."

"Thank you, Mano."

Fleming watched through the grimy window as Shaye destroyed the food on the table. After the initial conversation with the bartender, there was no more talking. Even if Shaye was asking the man about him and his brother, Harry, there was no problem. The Flemings had never stepped foot in the Cantina Rosita.

The more Red watched Thomas Shaye, the more convinced he became that the man was alone.

Easy pickings.

TWENTY-SIX

Sheriff Daniel Shaye ate his breakfast at his desk, thinking about his two sons. If not for the looming shadow of Cole Doucette, he'd be out on the trail with them, tracking the Fleming brothers. He probably wouldn't even have sent James after Candy. Rather, the three of them could have tracked the Flemings, figuring Candy would — at some point — join up with them. As it stood, Candy would probably lead James to the Flemings, but whether it would be before or after Thomas caught up to them was to be seen.

He left his office to carry the tray back to the café. When he walked in, Katrina smiled from across the room and then ran over to him.

"Any word, Sheriff?" she asked, taking the tray from him.

"From Thomas?" He shook his head. "Not a peep."

"Aren't you worried?"

"About my boys? They're deputies. They can take care of themselves."

"I'm sure they can," she said. "That's why you've got that new frown line between your eyes."

"Where?"

She pressed her forefinger to a spot on his forehead. "Right there."

"You're a crazy girl," he said.

"You should have had a telegram from Thomas or James by now," she insisted.

"Not if they have nothin' to say."

"How about telegraphing that they're still alive?"

"You worry too much, girl."

"And you don't worry enough, Dan Shaye!" she said, scolding him.

"As soon as I hear anythin', I promise to let you know."

"You'd better!"

Shaye turned and left the café.

He *was* worried about his boys, but he wasn't about to discuss his feelings with Katrina, or anyone else, for that matter. He'd been making his rounds twice as often as he usually did, just so he wouldn't sit in his office and wonder about his deputies. He knew Thomas could handle himself, but he was tracking two men, not one. As for

144

James, this was the first time he'd sent his youngest son out on his own. James was not the gunhand Thomas was, and frankly, was not as tough as his older brother.

He started walking his early rounds. Maybe he'd have some conversations with storekeepers or citizens, to keep his mind busy. He didn't need to be thinking about Thomas and James every minute of the day.

During Shaye's rounds, he'd been keeping a sharp eye on Main Street and any strangers riding into town. For the past week, nothing unusual had happened. Now, at midday, there he was, a single rider, coming down the street at a very leisurely pace.

He didn't doubt that Cole Doucette would send someone in ahead of him to take stock of the conditions in town. Once he found out the sheriff was there alone, without his deputies, that's when Doucette would be coming in.

Shaye watched the stranger until he'd reined in his horse in front of the Renegade Saloon. He tied his horse off and went inside.

Shaye crossed the street and entered the saloon, stopping just inside the batwing doors. The stranger stood at the bar, but didn't stay there long. He ordered a bottle, then turned and carried it and a glass to a nearby table. He sat alone with tables full of men clustered around him. That was what someone would do who wanted to gather intelligence about a town without actually asking questions.

Shaye had done some research on Cole Doucette and learned that the man had been an officer during the Civil War, for the Confederacy. As such, he'd be familiar with intelligence work.

Shaye walked over to the man's table, ignoring the greetings he got from some of the surrounding patrons. The Renegade was the busiest saloon in town, and even during "off" hours when people were working in stores or on a nearby ranch, there were customers.

He stopped at the stranger's table as the man was pouring himself a drink. When he finished, he set the bottle down, and then looked up at Shaye.

"Sheriff," the man said. "Can I help you?"

"Mind if I sit?"

"You're the law," the man said. "You'd sit whether I minded or not, wouldn't you?"

The man was intelligent. That was obvious from his speech pattern. Just the kind of man who'd be sent in to gather information. A stupid man would be useless for such work.

Shaye sat.

"Drink? I can get another glass."

"No, thanks. I saw you ride into town."

"And you thought you'd greet me personally," the stranger said. "I appreciate that."

"You got a name?"

"Everybody's got a name, Sheriff," the man said. "I bet you've got one."

"Sheriff Daniel Shaye."

"I've heard of you" the man said. "My name's Tate Kingdom."

Shaye sat back.

"I've heard of you, too."

"Well, luckily," Kingdom said, "I'm not wanted in Arizona. Or even the surrounding areas."

"So is that why you're here?" Shaye asked. "Because you're not wanted?"

"Not really," Kingdom said. "I just needed a bottle, is all."

"So you're on your way to somewhere else?"

"Look," Kingdom said, "I'm just trying to stay out of trouble."

"Well, a man with your reputation with a gun has trouble following him everywhere, don't you think?"

Kingdom laughed. "I don't know. But I guess a man with your reputation knows all about that."

"Men don't seek out the law as much as they seek out gunfighters," Shaye pointed out. "Killin' you will give a man a much bigger reputation than killin' me."

"I think you're too modest, Sheriff," Kingdom said.

"Tell me," Shaye said, "you know a man named Doucette?"

"Doucette?" Kingdom repeated. "Let me think. There was a Cole Doucette went to prison a few years ago."

"That's him."

"Is he out?"

"He is."

"What's that got to do with me?"

"He's on his way here."

"Again," Kingdom asked, "what's that got to do with me?"

"I figure he'll send an advance man to town to get the lay of the land."

"And you figure that's me?"

"I'm just lookin' at strangers comin' into town," Shaye said, "and you're the first one in days."

"Well, I'm sorry to disappoint you, Sheriff," Kingdom said. "I don't know Cole Doucette."

Shaye studied the man. He was in his mid-thirties, had been carrying that fast-gun

148

reputation with him for over ten years. He had an easy way about him, the kind men who can take care of themselves always have. Shaye knew Thomas was going to have that in a few years, maybe sooner.

"I guess I'm going to have to take your word for that, Mr. Kingdom."

"Oh, just call me Tate. Everybody does."

"Okay, Tate," Shaye said, "we're not going to have any problems in town if you're not with Doucette."

"No trouble from me, Sheriff," Kingdom said. "I'm just looking to drink, eat, sleep and maybe play a little poker."

"How long are you plannin' on stayin' in Vengeance Creek?" Shaye asked.

"Don't know," Kingdom said. "I guess that depends on how nice a town it is."

"Well, it's pretty nice, most times," Shaye said, "but if Doucette and his gang get here . . ."

"What are they coming here for?" Kingdom asked. "Do you know?"

"Revenge."

"Revenge in Vengeance Creek," Kingdom said, pouring himself another drink. "How fitting. Are you the target?"

"No," Shaye said. "I've never met the man, either."

"Well," Kingdom said, "I'm sure you and

your deputies can handle him and his gang."

"I guess that'll depend on how many men he comes with."

"And I guess that'll depend on whether he wants revenge against one man or the whole town."

That was a good point. If Doucette would be satisfied with just killing the mayor, he could even do it alone. But if he intended to make the whole town pay for what happened to him — figuring they deserved it for having Snow as the mayor — he'd come with enough men to take a town.

If that was the case, without Thomas and James, Shaye would be in a lot of trouble.

TWENTY-SEVEN

Shaye wasn't satisfied that Kingdom was not Doucette's advance man. But he didn't think he was. It wasn't the kind of job a man like Tate Kingdom hired out for. Kingdom was a money gun, pure and simple. This kind of job would be beneath him.

Shaye was sitting in a chair out in front of his office, thinking about making rounds again, when three riders galloped down the street. Strangers. Four in one day. That was unusual. Vengeance Creek wasn't exactly off the beaten path, but it wasn't on any kind of right of way, either.

He watched the three men ride up to the Renegade and dismount. Would Doucette send three of his men in ahead of him? Maybe to occupy Dan Shaye's time?

Shaye actually wouldn't have minded if these were Doucette's men. Maybe he could take care of them before their boss got there. It would give him that many less men to face with Cole Doucette.

But to find out if they worked for Doucette, he was going to have to ask them.

He got up from his chair and crossed the street to the Renegade Saloon.

The Renegade was in full swing when Shaye entered this time. It didn't look like there was an empty table to be had. On his way in, he passed two men stumbling out, one of whom looked like he had a broken arm.

"What happened, Jakes?" he asked the healthy one.

"Three strangers elbowed their way up to the bar and pushed Edwards here out of the way. When he protested, they broke his arm."

"Okay," Shaye said, "get him to the doc."

Jakes supported Edwards as they walked away from the saloon.

Shaye usually had good luck when confronting strangers in town. That was because most of them were just looking for a drink and a good time. Or, like the men Mayor Snow had brought in, they weren't prepared to fight.

The other kind of man was Tate Kingdom, who was relaxed right up to the moment he had to pull his gun.

As he entered the Renegade, he had no

idea what he might encounter at the hands of the three strangers, although Edwards's broken arm gave him ammo for a good guess.

They were standing at the bar, having forced their way in by pushing others aside. They had beers, and were slapping each other on the back.

Shaye approached, and some of the patrons at the bar who saw him coming made room for him.

"You fellas havin' a good time already?" he asked the three. "You just rode into town."

They looked over at him to see who was addressing them, spotting the badge on his shirt.

"Well, look here, Willy," one said. "The sheriff's come to greet us."

"I see 'im, Bama," Willy said. "Sheriff, let us buy you a drink."

"I'll need to know your names," Shaye said.

"To have a drink with us?"

"To know if you're wanted."

"Well, I'm Willy Raines," the spokesman said, "this here's Paul Grant, and that there's Bama."

Bama smiled. "They call me that 'cause I'm from Alabama."

Raines and Grant looked to be in their thirties, while Bama was a big man in his late twenties.

"You fellas always break somebody's arm the minute you get to town?" Shaye asked.

"Sure," Bama said, "sort of sets the tone, don't ya think? Nobody bothers us after that."

"Don't pay no attention to him, Sheriff," Willy said. "We didn't mean to break that fella's arm. He just sort of got in our way."

"Well, he's gonna need doctorin'," Shaye said, "and somebody's going to have to pay the doctor bill on that."

"Well, we'll pay it, Sheriff," Willy said. "No problem."

"Yeah," Bama said with a laugh. "You just have that fella bring us the bill."

"Then maybe we can break his other arm, huh, Bama?" Grant said, speaking for the first time.

"I'm gonna need you boys to come along with me," Shaye said.

"Where to, Sheriff?" Willy asked.

"My office."

"To jail?" Grant asked.

"That's right," Shaye said, "but first I'll need you to put your guns on the bar."

"Now, Sheriff," Willy Raines said, putting his beer mug down, "this seems a little excessive, don't ya, think? All we done was break a fella's arm."

The other two also put their mugs down. They all turned to face Shaye.

"That happens to be against the law in this town," Shaye said. "You'll need to spend a day in a cell."

"We ain't spendin' no time in a cell, Sheriff," Willy Raines said. "And I don't think you're man enough to take us over there. Not alone, anyways."

"And I don't see no deputies," Grant said. "You got deputies, Sheriff?"

"I don't need any deputies to handle three punks like you," Shaye said.

"Now, Sheriff," Willy said, "there ain't no need for name callin'. Bama don't like it when somebody calls him names."

"No," Bama said, "I sure don't."

"So, why don't you and Bama put your guns on the bar, and you two fellas can have it out, man to man," Willy suggested.

"That sounds doable," Shaye said. "You first, Bama."

"I don't need no gun to handle an old man," Bama said, dropping his gun onto the bar and stepping away.

Now that his gun was out of reach, Shaye had a two-on-one situation.

"Okay, now the two of you. Guns on the bar."

It suddenly got very quiet in the saloon, and a wide circle formed around the four men.

Raines frowned. "I thought you was gonna take on Bama man-to-man."

"Now what kind of jackass would I be to agree to that?" Shaye asked.

"You lied?" Willy asked.

"I didn't lie," Shaye said. "I said it sounded doable. Then I changed my mind."

"Why you —" Bama said, taking a step.

"Don't make me shoot an unarmed man, Bama," Shaye said.

Willy studied Shaye for a few moments, then said, "You know, I don't think you would, Sheriff."

"Ask Bama if he wants to test your theory."

"Besides," Willy went on, "I don't think you could get your gun out quick enough to do it before me and Paul got you."

"You're willlin' to shoot an officer of the law?" Shaye asked.

"Willin'," Willy said, "if you force our hand."

"He may not shoot an unarmed man," someone from the crowd in the saloon said, "but I would."

Willy, Grant and Bama looked to see who was speaking, but Shaye didn't have to look. He recognized the voice, even though he hadn't realized the man was still in the saloon.

"Who the hell are you?" Willy asked. He looked at Shaye. "I thought you didn't need any deputies."

"He ain't a deputy," Shaye said, "just a guest in town, like you."

Willy looked at the man again. "I asked you a question, mister. Who're you and why are you buttin' in where you don't belong."

"Well," the man said, "I'm buttin' in because the sheriff looked like he could use some help. See, without me, he'd end up having to kill the three of you."

"That so?" Willy asked.

"That's Dan Shaye you're bad-mouthing, friend. If you don't know who he is, you ought to."

"And you ain't told me who you are, yet."

"The name's Kingdom."

Willy's eyebrows went up, and both Grant and Bama fidgeted.

"Tate Kingdom?"

"That's right."

Willy licked his lips. "We didn't know you was in town, Mr. Kingdom."

"Well, you know now."

"What about it, boys?" Shaye asked. "You gonna put your guns on the bar or not?"

Willy looked away from Tate and at Shaye. "Sure, Sheriff," he said. "Sure, we're gonna put our guns on the bar."

He and Grant hurriedly took their guns out of their holsters and set them on the bar.

"Lyle," Shaye said to the bartender, "you mind puttin' those under your bar? I'll come and get 'em when I get a chance."

"Sure thing, Sheriff." Lyle scooped them off the bar and hid them away.

"Now we're gonna walk over to the jail and get you boys situated," Shaye said. He still hadn't pulled his gun, and when he looked at Kingdom, the gunfighter's gun was still in his holster. "You comin'?"

"I think you can handle three unarmed men, Sheriff," Kingdom said, "don't you? I've got an unfinished drink here."

"Then maybe you can stop over for a talk when you finish that drink," Shaye said.

"I'll make a point of it, Sheriff."

Shaye looked at the three men and said, "Let's go."

TWENTY-EIGHT

Shaye put the three men into three separate cells.

"How long do you intend to keep us here, Sheriff?" Willy Raines asked.

"I don't know," Shaye said. "I guess that'll depend on how soon Doucette gets here."

"Who?" Bama asked.

"What's Cole Doucette got to do with us?" Willy asked.

"You know him?"

"I heard of him," Raines admitted.

"Well, he's on his way here," Shaye said, "and I've been expectin' him to send some advance men into town."

"And you think that's us?" Grant asked.

"I'm askin' if it's you."

"If it is," Raines said, "would we tell you?"

"If you want to get out of these cells," Shaye said, "ever."

"You can't keep us here!" Bama said, gripping the bars of his cell tightly.

159

Shaye looked at him. "I can make sure you die in these cells."

"Okay, look," Raines said, "we're not workin' for Cole Doucette. We're just passin' through."

"Are you wanted?" Shaye asked.

"Not here," Raines said. "Not in Arizona. You have no reason to hold us."

"You broke a man's arm," Shaye said.

"We'll pay his doctor bill," Raines said. "And leave town. You won't ever see us again."

Shaye turned to leave the cell block.

"Hey!" Raines shouted.

"I'll let you know what I decide in the mornin'," Shaye said, closing the cell block door.

"Can we at least get some food?" Grant yelled.

As Shaye turned, the door opened and Tate Kingdom walked in, carrying three gunbelts.

"I thought I'd save you a trip back to the saloon," he said, dropping the guns on Shaye's desk.

"Thanks," Shaye said. He swept the three gunbelts into a desk drawer. "And thanks for your help over there."

"Well," Kingdom said, "I couldn't just

stand by and watch you gun those men down."

"And you were sure that was what would happen?" Shaye asked. "You didn't think you might be savin' my life?"

"Well, maybe," Kingdom said, "but my money would've been on you."

He sat down in front of the desk, while Shaye sat himself down behind it.

"What'd you want to see me about?" Kingdom asked.

"I have an idea," Shaye said. "These men don't seem to be workin' for Doucette, but he is on his way here."

"With how many men?"

"That I don't know."

"And you don't have any deputies?"

"My sons are my deputies, and they're . . . away."

"When do you expect them back?"

"I don't know," Shaye said. "When their jobs are done, I suppose."

"So they're . . . what? Chasing someone?"

"Yes," Shaye said, "they're each tracking a killer."

"Ah . . ."

"So I could probably use your help again."

Kingdom kept his hands in his lap and studied Shaye.

"You're satisfied I'm not working for Dou-

161

cette, and they're not working for Doucette?"

"I'm choosin' to believe that you don't," Shaye said. "You don't strike me as that kind of man."

"Why?"

"It's too menial a task for you."

"For a man of my . . . what? Ego?"

"Reputation."

Kingdom put his feet up on Shaye's desk. "And what about them?"

"Whether they work for him or not, they're in cells, and tomorrow they'll be out of town."

"If they are working for him, they'll go back and tell what they know."

"Which is what?" Shaye asked. "They were here five minutes, and then I threw them in a cell."

"They know about me."

"But not about my sons," Shaye said. "As far as Doucette will know, he'll have to deal with us, and with you."

"So four against . . . how many." It wasn't a question, really.

Shaye decided to confide in Kingdom.

"Doucette is comin' to kill the mayor."

"Why?"

"He's the lawyer who convicted him and put him away."

"What about the judge who convicted him?"

Shaye shrugged. "Maybe he'll be next. Or maybe Doucette's already killed him. My concern is the mayor — actually, it's the town."

"So let him kill the mayor, and maybe he'll leave."

"I can't do my job that selectively," Shaye replied. "I've got to watch out for all the people in town."

"That's a lot for one man."

"Well," Shaye said, "maybe he won't get here until my sons are back."

Kingdom dropped his feet to the floor and stood up.

"I guess I'll be around for a while. Let me know if you need me."

"I don't suppose you'd wear a badge?"

Kingdom gave him a look. "What do you think?"

He walked out.

"I didn't think so," Shaye said, to himself.

TWENTY-NINE

James decided not to catch up to Candy.

When he realized he could catch him, he had second thoughts. Why not keep tracking him, following him, until he rejoined the Fleming brothers? He was not the tracker his father or brother were, but he was enough of one to know he was a few hours behind the man.

At first he thought the meeting would be happening in Tucson, but when the tracks made it clear that Candy had bypassed the large town, he figured they'd be meeting someplace smaller.

Like, perhaps, Tubac, about fifty miles farther south. Or maybe he was on his way to Mexico.

But even before Tubac, James followed the trail to a gathering of buildings that didn't look like a town or a ranch. Perhaps a settlement of some kind.

He reined in his horse within sight of the

buildings, careful not to be seen. While he watched, several people walked or ran between the buildings, but he never saw Candy or the man's horse. Behind one of the buildings was a corral with three horses in it, but Candy's wasn't one of them.

He finally decided to ride down and have a look. He guided his horse at an easy pace, so as not to spook anybody. As he approached, a woman came out of one of the buildings, which now looked like shacks. She was wearing a long blue dress that covered her from neck to ankles.

"Hello," he called out.

She waved with one hand. The other hand was out of sight. As he got closer he saw that she didn't look happy, and he saw something red on her dress. It was a stain, like . . . blood.

Abruptly, she brought her other hand around and pointed a gun at him.

"Need help with that?" he asked, showing her his empty hands. "I'm not here to threaten you in any way."

"That's what the other man said," she replied.

"What other man?"

From behind him he heard a man say, "Your friend, who rode through here earlier."

James turned his head and saw a man holding a rifle pointed at him. He raised his hands a little higher.

"I don't have a friend out here," he said, "but I am tracking somebody. A killer."

"We can believe that," the man said. "That he's a killer. Climb off your horse — but first toss your gun down."

"Now look —"

"Do it!"

James plucked his gun from his holster and dropped it to the ground.

"Now the rifle."

He tossed the rifle after the pistol.

"Okay, now dismount."

He did so, slowly.

"Turn around. Face me, not her."

He looked at the woman, who he now saw was a girl, and a frightened one. Then he turned to face the man. At that moment, the man with the rifle saw the badge.

"Where's that badge from?"

"Vengeance Creek."

"I don't know it."

"It's a little northwest of here," James said. "No reason why you should have heard of it."

"What are you doin' out here?" the man asked.

"I told you," James said, "I'm a deputy,

tracking a killer."

"And how do we know you ain't a killer carryin' a badge?" the man asked.

"Well," James said, "all I've got is my word. I can't offer any more than that."

"This killer got a name?"

"Cannaday," James said. "Dan Cannaday, but they call him Candy."

"He told me to call him Candy, Pa," the girl said.

"Quiet, girl."

"I think he's tellin' the truth, Pa."

"Girl, I told you —"

"That man shot my brother, Deputy," the girl said. "Can you help him?"

"I can try," James said. "I've patched my own brother up a time or two."

"Glory —" the man said.

"Eddie needs help, Pa!" she said.

The man with the rifle looked to be in his fifties and kept flexing his hands on the rifle nervously.

"Mister," James said, "just don't get nervous with that gun, and I'll see what I can do. I don't need my guns. You can leave them out here on the ground."

"I'll pick 'em up," the man said. "But yeah, okay, let's go inside."

"This way," the girl said, finally lowering the gun. "Please hurry!"

167

She led him to the shack she had come out of. He heard the man behind him pick up his guns and follow.

As he entered the building, he saw a boy about fifteen years old, bleeding from what looked like a belly wound. He was lying on his back on a cot, and somebody had made an attempt to bandage him.

"Candy did this?" James asked.

"Yes," the girl said. "He rode in, said he wanted to trade horses. We negotiated some money, also, so he went to look at what we had in the corral. When he saw them he got angry, pulled his gun. They weren't worth tradin' for, he said."

"He thought we had other horses some-where else," the man said, taking up the story. "We told him we didn't, but he thought we were lying. He . . . he shot my son, to make a point."

James got down on his knees next to the boy's cot. His face was pale and sweaty, his eyes shiny.

"Then what happened?"

"He finally believed us," the girl said, "and he rode on."

James wondered why, if Candy shot the boy, he didn't shoot them, as well. He moved the boy's shirt, and the makeshift bandage, to examine the wound. He had lied to them. He'd never treated Thomas for a gunshot, but he had watched his father do it.

The wound wasn't as bad as he first thought. The bullet hadn't hit him in the belly, but the side. Still, the bullet would have to come out.

"How is he?" the father asked.

"Not as bad as he looks," James said, "but the bullet has to come out." He glanced at them over his shoulder. "Has either of you ever done it? Removed a bullet?"

"No," the man said.

"Can you do it?" the girl asked. "Can you save him?"

"Isn't there anyone else here?" he asked. "In the other buildings."

"Nobody," the man said. "You'll have to do it."

"Look," James said, sticking to his lie, "I've only done it a couple of times —"

The man raised his rifle and pointed it at James again. From the look on his face, he meant business. The girl was another story. She didn't like the situation, at all.

"So you'll do it one more time," he said. "But remember, if he dies, you die."

"Pa!" the girl said. "That's not fair."

"It's not fair that your brother got shot," the father said. "That man came here

169

because this man is chasin' him. I blame them both."

James thought the girl was right. That wasn't fair, not at all.

THIRTY

James asked the girl if she could get him water and clean bandages. She said she could.

"And a fire?" he asked.

"What for?" the man said.

James took out his Bowie knife. "I need this to be held in a fire before I can use it to dig out the bullet."

"That'll kill him!"

"You got something smaller?" James asked.

The man shook his head.

"I'll get it hot," the girl said, taking the knife.

"I'm gonna need your help," James told the man.

"For what?"

"I'm gonna need you to hold him still while I dig for the bullet."

The man seemed conflicted. If he did that, who would hold the rifle on James?

171

"Come on!" James snapped. "Put the rifle down. I'm not goin' anywhere!"

With great reluctance the man put the rifle aside and went to the cot.

"Get on the other side," James said. "I need you to talk to him, keep him calm, and then hold him down while I get the bullet out."

"Are you sure you can do that?" the man asked.

"No, I'm not," James said, "but you didn't ask me that before."

The girl returned holding a basin of water, some bandages, and the knife.

"Is this okay?"

She handed James the knife, which was hot.

"It'll have to be."

He tore the boy's shirt away and discarded the bandage she'd applied.

"What should I do?" she asked.

"Just squat down beside me and hold the basin and the bandages."

She did as he asked, careful not to spill the water. James washed his hands in the basin, finding the water to be as hot as the knife. There had to be a stove or a campfire someplace.

"Okay," he said. "I'll need to clean away

172

some of the blood so I can see what I'm do-ing."

He soaked one cloth she gave him and used it to clean the wound. Once he had a good view of the entry hole, he was able to dig for the bullet. Luckily, it wasn't very deep. He had the girl continue to clean blood from the wound, and the father hold the boy down so he couldn't move around too much. Finally, he had the bullet and dropped it into the pan of water.

"Now we've got to get this bandaged so the bleedin' stops," he said.

Using the makeshift bandages Glory had given him, he bandaged the boy nice and tight, hoping the bandage would stem the red tide.

"There," James said, standing up, "that should do it."

"Is he gonna be all right?" Glory asked.

"I hope so," James said.

The father remained on his knees next to his son. At least he wasn't picking up the rifle again.

"Can I get some clean water to wash my hands with?" James asked.

"Oh, I'll get some more from the pump," Glory offered.

"Never mind," James said. "Just show me where the pump is."

"It's out back," she said. "I'll take you."

She grabbed the basin and led the way. As they went out the back door, she dumped the bloody water, then led him to the pump.

"Thanks," James said. He pumped some clear water and cleaned the blood from his hands. She handed him a cloth to dry with, then rinsed out the basin.

"Is your father gonna shoot me with his rifle?" he asked.

"I don't think so," she said. "I hope not."

The sun shone off her golden hair, and he could see she was barely eighteen.

"How old is your brother?"

"Fifteen."

"Is it just you, your brother and father here?"

"Yes," she said. "We found this place a couple of months ago after we lost our ranch. All we had were those three horses in the corral."

"So you're stayin' here?"

"For now."

"What about the owners?"

"We never saw any owners."

If there were owners and they returned, this family would be considered squatters.

"Did Candy get anythin' from you?" he asked, changing the subject.

"He took some food," she said. "And

he . . . touched me."

"Touched you?"

"He grabbed me, ran his hands over . . . that was when he shot Eddie. He tried to make Candy let me go."

"I thought it was when he saw the horses."

"He was mad about the horses," she said, "and then he grabbed me and . . . said he was gonna get somethin' out of us. Eddie ran at him, even though Pa tried to stop him. So that man . . . Candy . . . shot him."

"Then what?'

"Then he took some food and lit out."

"I'm wonderin' . . ." James said.

"What?" she asked, eyes all wide.

"I'm wonderin' why he didn't kill you all."

"I don't know," she said, "but gee, I'm glad he didn't."

"Let's go back inside before your Pa comes lookin' for me with his rifle again."

They went back into the house, where her father was still hovering over his son.

"Eddie was askin' about you," her father said.

"I'm here, Eddie," she said, crouching down next to him.

"Am I — am I okay?" he asked.

"Yeah, you are, brother," Glory said. "This man took the bullet out and patched you up."

"Thanks, mister."

"Sure thing," James said. He looked at their father. "Okay if I take my guns and go? I've got to catch up to Candy."

"You catch up to him," the man said, "and you kill him for me, mister. You put a bullet in him and tell him it's from Josh Kramer."

"And Eddie," Glory said.

"I'll tell him," James promised, picking up his gun.

He had slid his rifle back into its scabbard and was about to mount his horse when Glory came running out.

"You never told me your name?" she complained.

"It's James," he said, "Deputy James Shaye."

"Well, Deputy James," she said, "are you sure you won't stay a bit. I'm gonna make some stew for Eddie, and I'm a pretty fair cook."

"It sounds real good, Glory," he said, "but I really have to try and catch up to Candy."

"He's a real mean man, James," she said. "Are you sure you can handle him?"

"I'll handle him," James said, "don't worry about that. Say, how far am I from Tubac?"

"It's about twenty miles," she said. "You

think he was headed there? It's pretty deserted."

"He's probably headed to Old Mexico," James said, "but I'll check Tubac, just to be sure."

Abruptly, she rushed to him and gave him a big hug, which embarrassed him.

"Stop by on your way back," she said. "Will you?"

"Okay, Glory," he said, mounting up, "I'll stop by on my way back."

THIRTY-ONE

He made Tubac as it was getting dark.

As Glory had told him, the town looked completely deserted. But he saw smoke coming from the chimney of one building and, as he approached it, he smelled something cooking.

He reined in his horse in front of the building, which appeared to be a cantina. Mounting the boardwalk, he paused to look around, didn't see any other horses or people, then went inside.

There was a fat Mexican behind the bar, and a pretty, dark-haired woman in her forties, wearing an apron and a peasant blouse. She looked Mexican, but somehow James didn't think she was.

"Hello," he said.

"Buenos Dias," she greeted. "We didn't expect anyone to be ridin' in this late."

"I smelled somethin' cookin'."

She smiled. "There's always somethin'

cookin', friend. Have a seat if you're hungry." When she spoke, it became obvious she wasn't Mexican.

"I am, ma'am," he said, "very hungry. But I need to know if anyone else has ridden into town today."

She squinted at his chest. "Seems to me I've seen one of those before."

"My badge?" he said. "When?"

"Seems like it was two days ago, another fella rode through here and stopped for a meal."

"A badge exactly like this one?"

She leaned in. "I think so."

"Did he say his name?"

"He did," she answered, "but I don't remember — was it Thomas?"

"Thomas Shaye?"

"That was him!"

"He's my brother," James said. "I'm James."

"Well," she said, putting her hands on her hips, "it seems like good looks run in the family."

"Did he say where he was goin'?"

"He was trackin' two men who had been here before him," she replied. "They were all goin' to Nogales."

"How far away is that?"

"Maybe twenty miles." She reached out

and put her hand on his arm. "But you don't want to ride in the dark. And you said you were hungry. Why not have a meal and spend the night. You can get an early start tomorrow."

"Well," he said, "I am pretty tired. Are you sure another man didn't ride in today before me?"

"No," she said, "nobody. Are you trackin' somebody other than the two your brother is trackin'?"

"Yes," he said, "but they did what they did together. I figure they're meetin' up."

"Well, if they do," she said, "perhaps you will meet your brother. Have a seat, I'll bring some food. And beer?"

"Yes, please."

"You Shaye men," she said, stroking his cheek as he sat, "handsome and polite."

She went into the kitchen to get the food, and while she was there the bartender came over with a mug of beer.

"Thank you," James said.

"Por nada, señor."

Moments later the woman came out and, after covering the table with a frayed cloth, laid out plates of meat, vegetables, rice and tortillas.

"Sure smells good," he said.

"Eat as much as you want," she said.

"There is a room in the back for you."

"You're very kind," he said.

"Not so kind," she said. "I'll be chargin' you."

"Don't worry," he told her. "I can pay."

"I'm not worried," she assured him.

After eating enough to fill his belly twice over, James allowed the woman — she said her name was Irma — to show him to his room. It was small, but clean. The floor creaked as they moved around, as it had in the hallway.

"Thank you, Miss Irma."

She touched the scooped neck of her blouse and said, "I could come back a little later, keep you company."

"And there'd be a charge for that, too?" he asked.

"Well, of course."

"That's okay, then," James said. "I'll just get some sleep. I need to start early in the mornin'."

"After breakfast?" she asked.

"Coffee will be fine," he said. "Good-night."

"Good-night, James. I'll be out front or down the hall, if you change your mind during the night and want a warm body next to you."

He leaned out and watched her walk down the hall — stepping on the creaky boards along the way — then closed the door. Sitting on the bed, he removed his boots. He hated the idea of being two days behind Thomas, but Irma was right about one thing. It wouldn't be smart to try to ride at night.

If Candy bypassed Tubac, he was probably camped between there and Nogales. James would push his mount the next morning, get to Nogales before noon.

He reclined on the bed and tried to get to sleep.

Sometime during the night James woke. He frowned, wondering what had awakened him, then realized what it was. That creaky floorboard in the hall. He grabbed his gun from the holster on the bedpost and got off the bed. He crouched next to it and waited, with his eyes on the door. There was just enough moonlight through the window for him to see that there was light coming from beneath the door from a lamp in the hall. As he watched, the shadow of two feet appeared beneath the door.

James held his gun ready as somebody touched the doorknob. Slowly, the door began to open, and by the light from the hall, he saw a gun. He forced himself to wait, and when the man was inside the room, he fired. The bullet struck the shadow of the man and drove him out into the hall.

James ran for the door, gun ready, but he didn't need another shot. Candy lay in the hall, dead.

"Irma?" James called. He wondered if she'd been working with Candy. "I'm comin' down the hall, Irma."

He moved down the hallway with his gun at the ready, checked the other rooms and found them empty. Stepping into the cantina, he found that empty, as well. That left the kitchen. He went there and looked in. Tied up and gagged on the floor were Irma and her bartender, who looked as if he'd also been pistol-whipped.

He holstered his gun and set about untying them.

"Are you all right?" he asked.

"I'm so sorry," Irma said, "but when you got here, he was in the kitchen with his gun. I couldn't warn you. He said he'd kill us."

"That's okay," James said. "He's dead now."

"Is he the man you were chasin'?" she asked, as he helped her to her feet.

"Yes, he was," James said. "I was hopin' he'd lead me to the others."

"What will you do now?" she asked.

"Well, you take care of him," he said, indicating the battered and bruised bartender, "and I'll get the body out of here. Then we'll try to get some sleep, and I'll head out come mornin'. Maybe I can catch up to my brother before he catches up to the others."

"But you're two days behind him."

"I'll push my horse," James said. "I have to try."

"Thank you," she said, "for helpin' us."

"That's okay," James said. "Take care of your bartender, and I'll dump the body. Maybe my brother and I will stop here on the way back and pick it up."

"A-all right," she said. "Would you like a drink when you come back in?"

"Actually, yeah," he said. "I'd really like a drink."

The next morning James woke to a full Mexican breakfast, which Irma insisted he eat before leaving.

"You saved us last night," she said. "We owe you somethin'."

"*Si, señor,*" the bartender said, bringing over a pot of coffee.

So he ate and washed it down with the coffee, then went out to saddle his horse,

184

which he had left in a deserted livery stable the night before.

When he rode back past the cantina, Irma was standing outside.

"Remember," she called out to him, "you and your brother come back."

He waved.

"Good luck!" she called after him.

Now that he had no trail to follow, James simply gave the horse his spurs and rode hell-bent-for-leather for Nogales. He hoped that he would not only find his brother there, but find him alive.

THIRTY-TWO

James reached Nogales on the American side on an exhausted horse — and it was not yet dusk. He rode directly to the sheriff's office and dismounted. As he entered, a man with tired eyes sitting behind the desk looked up at him, surprised.

"Help you, stranger?" he asked.

"You the sheriff?"

"That's me." The man pointed to the star on his chest. "Frank Dewey's my name."

"Well, I'm James Shaye, deputy from Vengeance Creek. I'm trackin' two men, the Fleming Brothers, and my brother, Thomas. He's also a deputy."

"Have a seat, son," Dewey said.

"I don't have time —"

"You'll have time for this," Dewey said. "I guarantee it."

James frowned, but sat down.

"I'm afraid I have some bad news for you," Dewey said. "We just got the word

186

from Nogales, across the border."

"What word is that, Sheriff?"

"Your brother," Dewey said, "he's dead."

"What?" James felt cold inside.

"Seems the Flemings shot him."

"How?" James asked. "In the back?"

"Face-to-face," Dewey said. "In the street. At least, that's what people are sayin'."

James jumped to his feet.

"That can't be," he said. "My brother's alive."

"Why would you say that?" Dewey asked.

"Because those two wouldn't have been able to take Thomas in a fair fight," James said. "He's too fast."

"Well," Dewey said, "Red Fleming is supposed to be pretty quick with a gun, himself . . . and there were two of them."

"I don't care," James said. "I won't believe my brother's dead until I see the body."

"You'd have to go across the border for that. You'd have no jurisdiction, and you might end up dead, too."

"How's that?"

"The Flemings are still there."

"So they're supposed to have killed my brother," James said, "and they didn't leave town?"

"Like I said," Dewey answered, "you and your brother have no jurisdiction over there, so it's not like they killed a lawman."

"As far as I'm concerned," James said, "a lawman's a lawman, no matter where he goes."

"Okay," Dewey said. "Okay, sit back down a minute."

James sat.

"You wanna ride right over there and find out what happened?"

"I do."

"Well, be smart about it," Dewey said.

"How do I do that?"

"First, take off your badge and put it in your pocket," Dewey said. "Second, don't let anybody in this town know you're the other deputy's brother. Third, keep your head down. There are people in this town who will send the Flemings a message if they learn you're a deputy, and then the Flemings will know you're comin'. Fourth, there's a sheriff over there named Montoya. He can't be trusted."

"He works for the Flemings?"

"He works for himself," Dewey said, "as I do. But I wouldn't trust him to do the right thing."

"And you?"

"Me? I do the right thing about half the time. I have a gambling habit."

"I see. You're very honest."

Dewey smiled. "Like I said, half the time."

"So what do you suggest I do?" James asked.

"Nothin' abrupt," Dewey said. "Somebody saw you ride into town. You're a stranger. What somebody would normally do is have a drink, maybe a steak, and spend the night. Tomorrow mornin' you can head over the border at a real leisurely pace."

"Tomorrow? But —"

"If you're brother is really dead, he'll still be dead tomorrow. If he's still alive, what's the hurry?"

"If he's still alive," James said, "I want him to stay that way."

"You can both stay that way as long as you don't attract the wrong attention. Look, just do it my way for today. Tomorrow you can go across the border and find out."

"Can you find anythin' out for sure before then?" James asked.

"I can try."

"Is there a telegraph office in town?"

"Yes, but not across the border."

"I was just thinkin' of sendin' one back to Vengeance Creek."

"Well," Dewey said, "you don't wanna tell your father anythin' until you know for sure."

"You're right." James stood up. "Do you

have suggestions for a place to drink, eat and stay?"

"I have a few."

THIRTY-THREE

James checked into a hotel, then went across the street to the saloon for a beer. According to Sheriff Dewey, these were places Thomas went while he was in town.

"What else did he do?" James had asked.

"He talked to a girl named Belle at the saloon across from the hotel," Dewey said. "And also a man named Adam Grey, a gambler in town."

"What else is Grey besides a gambler?" James asked.

"I'm sure he sent word across the border to the Flemings that your brother was comin'."

"Why are you tellin' me this?"

"Because I want you to stay away from these two people," Dewey said.

But James wanted to at least have a look at this Belle, and maybe even Grey.

The saloon was busy, so he walked to the bar without attracting attention. His badge was in his pocket, as Dewey had suggested.

He ordered a beer, then looked around while he drank it. There was some gambling going on — poker and faro — but nobody who matched the description Dewey had given him for Adam Grey. However, he immediately spotted Belle. Dewey had described her perfectly. For one thing, she was older than the other girls.

He watched as she moved around the saloon, talking to customers, serving drinks. He wanted to ask her about Thomas, but he decided Sheriff Dewey was right about not calling attention to himself.

He finished his beer, left the saloon and went to the restaurant Dewey had suggested. When he walked in, he saw Dewey sitting there at a table, eating alone. The lawman waved him over.

"Have a seat," he invited.

"Is that what you call keepin' my head down?" James asked. "Eating with the local law?"

Dewey smiled. "I eat with a lot of people. Siddown. You're attractin' more attention just standin' there."

James sat.

"Bring my guest a steak," Dewey told the waiter when he came over. "Rare okay?" he asked James.

"Fine."

"See that table in the center of the room?"

"The one with two men?"

"Yeah," Dewey said, "the older one is Adam Grey, the gambler."

"And the younger one?"

"Just a business associate of his. Not important."

"Oh. Why are you pointin' him out? So I can stay away from him?"

"No," Dewey said, "because from what I've learned, he'll be the only person who can tell you if your brother is really dead."

James looked over at Grey. "I see."

"If you wanna ask him," Dewey said. "I mean, if you don't wanna wait to go across the border tomorrow and find out for yourself."

"So I walk over there and ask just ask him, out of the blue?"

"You could do that," Dewey said. "Or we could eat first. He hasn't even ordered yet."

Hunger pangs gnawed at James's stomach, so he said, "I think maybe we can eat first."

"Good choice," Dewey said.

James and Dewey finished their steaks well before Adam Grey and his companion finished theirs.

"Are you going to come over with me?"

James asked.

"No, I can't do that," Dewey said. "I still have to live in this town."

"Gotcha." James pushed his seat back. "So all that stuff about not callin' attention to myself?"

"I also heard that the Flemings rode out of Nogales today," Dewey said. "So Grey won't be able to send word that you're comin'."

"Understood." He started to stand up.

"By the way," Dewey said.

"Yeah?"

"You can put your badge back on if you like, just to make your point."

Thirty-Four

When James walked over to Adam Grey's table, he was wearing his badge. Not that it meant much, since he had no jurisdiction in Nogales on either side of the border. But it made him feel better.

As he stood in front of the man, Grey's companion looked up at him.

"Adam Grey?" he asked.

"That's right." Grey squinted at James's badge. "You're a little out of you bailiwick, aren't you, Deputy?"

"I think you met my brother," James said. "Also a deputy. Thomas Shaye?"

Grey frowned. "I think I might have —"

"Mind if I sit?" James pulled out a chair and dropped into it.

"Sam, why don't you take a walk," Grey said to the other man.

"I haven't finished —"

"Sam!"

"Yeah, okay." Sam stood up. "Don't let

195

the waiter take my plate."

"I'll keep an eagle eye on it," James promised, even though Sam wasn't talking to him.

"What's on your mind, Deputy?"

"I understand you might have some information for me."

"What kind of information?"

"About my brother."

"Can you be more specific?"

James leaned forward. "Is he dead or alive?"

"Ah . . ."

"I'm told you're the only one on this side of the border who really knows."

"I think you've been misinformed," Grey said. "I don't know anything about what goes on over there."

"Then I'll tell you," James said. "Supposedly, the Fleming brothers shot and killed him. If I get over there and find out that's true, I'm going to hunt them down, and then I'll be comin' back here for you."

"For me?" Grey asked. "That hardly sounds fair. What did I do?"

"I know you have a connection to them," James said. "Apparently you warned them that Thomas was comin'. And you'd warn them about me, except that they've left Nogales."

"Have they?" Grey asked.

"That's the word."

"You seem to have more information than a young man who just arrived in town should have," Grey said. "Possibly from your supper companion?"

"Sheriff Dewey was actually warnin' me to keep away from you," he lied, covering for the local lawman.

"That was good advice."

"I'm warnin' you, Grey, no matter what the sheriff says," James said, "if I find out you had information and you withheld it from me, I'll be back for you."

"That badge doesn't get you any privileges around here, son," Grey said. "If I was you, that's the thing I'd remember."

James was in a quandary. When he stood up, should he walk back to Dewey's table or just walk out? Make it look like he's mad at both Dewey and Grey, further covering for Dewey?

"We're done here," Grey said. "I'd like to finish my supper."

James stood.

"If you see Sam out there, send him in, will you?" Grey asked.

James decided his best course of action would be to just walk out of the restaurant. Dewey had helped him, and he didn't want to damage the man's credibility in his town any more than he had to.

The waiter came over as James started to leave, obviously mistook him for Sam, and asked, "Is the gentleman finished?"

"Yes," James said, "you can remove the plate."

James had no choice after that but to go back to his hotel. He didn't want to be seen with Sheriff Dewey anymore, and didn't want to run into Adam Grey again.

He was sitting in his room, stewing about Thomas. If his brother was, indeed, dead he'd have to send his father a telegram to that fact. If he did, however, he knew his father would message him back to return to Vengeance Creek immediately. James was not about to do that, not if Thomas was dead at the hands of the Fleming brothers and they were still on the loose. So he wouldn't send his father such a telegram. Hopefully, he'd never have to. To that end, he decided Thomas was not dead. He couldn't be. He'd find out tomorrow when he crossed the border to Nogales on the Mexican side that his brother was still alive and well.

He considered going to sleep so he could get a very early start in the morning when there was a knock on the door. Figuring the only person it could be was the sheriff, he nevertheless took his gun to the door with him. After all, Adam Grey could be sending somebody for him, after his threat — or promise — to the man.

"Who is it?"

"My name is Belle, Deputy," a woman's voice said. "Please, I must speak to you. Sheriff Dewey told me where you were stayin'."

James opened the door carefully, just a crack, and peered out. He saw the woman from the saloon he'd assumed was Belle.

"What do you want?" he asked, opening the door.

"Oh, please," she said, "let me in before somebody sees me."

"Worried about your reputation?" he asked.

"Worried about stayin' alive if Adam Grey finds out I came here to talk to you."

James made a quick decision.

"All right, come in." He stepped back, allowed her to enter, and closed the door. "Now, why are you here?"

"You're that deputy's brother, right? His name was Thomas?" she asked, anxiously.

"That's right. I'm James."

"Are you goin' across the border tomorrow?"

"That's right, I am. Did your boss send you to talk me out of it?"

"I told you," she said. "He doesn't know I'm here. And I don't want him to find out."

"Then why are you here?"

"To tell you," she said, "to let you know that your brother is alive. Thomas is alive!"

THIRTY-FIVE

"Are you sure?" James asked.

"Positive."

"How do you know?"

"I heard Adam talkin' about it," she said. "A man came here from across the border, told him there was a shooting, that your brother was involved, that he was shot, but he wasn't dead."

"And the Flemings?"

"Oh, they shot him," she said. "That's all I heard."

James sat down on the bed, put the gun in his holster hanging on the bedpost.

"When was that?" he asked.

"Just yesterday."

"So Thomas was still alive yesterday."

"Yes."

"And today the sheriff heard that the Flemings rode out," James said.

"I wouldn't believe everythin' the sheriff tells you."

"Does he work for Grey?"

"No," she said, "but he owes him money. That might be the same thing."

"As far as I can see, the sheriff has only done right by me, so far."

"Well," she said, "if I was you, I wouldn't believe anybody."

"Does that include you?"

"It does," she said, "but I'm only tellin' you what I heard. You'll find out for yourself tomorrow who's tellin' the truth."

She was right. Once he got to Nogales on the Mexico side, he'd know for sure who the liars were.

"Miss Belle —"

"Just Belle," she said.

"Belle, thanks for comin' here tonight," James said. "One way or the other, I'll be back through here, hopefully with my brother."

"I hope so," she said. "This town would be much better off without Adam Grey. Maybe one of you will kill him."

"Or arrest him," James said.

"Whichever," she said. "I should get back to my room."

He walked her to the door.

"Are you Grey's woman?" he asked.

"I owe him a lot of money, too," she explained, "so I'm his woman when he

202

wants me to be."

"I understand."

He opened the door for her.

"One more thing," he said.

"Yes?"

"Why'd you come here tonight to tell me this?"

"Like I said," she replied, "this town would be better off without Adam Grey. I'm hopin' he did somethin' to piss you Shaye boys off."

"Time will tell," he said.

THIRTY-SIX

James rode into Nogales on the Mexico side the next morning.

There was quite a difference between the two, but he wasn't interested in the comparison at that moment. What he was interested in was the sheriff's office.

"Montoya's his name," Dewey had told him the day before. "You can probably trust him as much as you can trust me."

Which wasn't much, James thought.

James dismounted and entered the office without knocking. It was early, not yet *siesta* time, still his entry brought Sheriff Montoya's boots down off his desk with a bang.

"Are you Sheriff Montoya?" James asked.

"*Si, señor,*" Montoya said, "that is my name. What can I do for you?"

"I'm lookin' for my brother."

"And who is your *hermano, señor?*"

"Deputy Sheriff Thomas Shaye." James took his badge out of his pocket and dropped it on the man's desk. "I'm Deputy James Shaye."

Montoya picked up the badge and looked at it.

"It is a very nice badge, *señor,*" he said, handing it back, "but it means nothing here."

"That's why I'm not depending on my badge to get me what I want," James said.

"And what is the *señor* depending on?"

"My gun. Do you want me to take that out, too?"

"No, no, *señor,*" Montoya said, "no guns. *Por favor,* not this early in the day. If you want your brother, I will take you to him."

Montoya stood up, strapped on his gun, and grabbed his hat from the peg on the wall.

"Vamanos," he said. "Follow me, please."

"If you're takin' me into some kind of trap . . ." James warned.

"Aieee," Montoya said, "you are as mistrustful as your brother. *Por favor, señor,* no trap. I assume you are also searching for the Fleming brothers?"

"That's right."

"Well, they are gone," Montoya said. "There is no danger, no trap. Will you follow me?"

"Lead the way," James said.

"Excelente," Montoya said. "This way, please."

They left the office and Montoya took the lead. James followed, pulling his horse by the reins.

When James saw that they were approaching what appeared to be the undertaker's, his heart almost stopped.

"Why here?" he asked, when they stopped in front.

"You will see."

James tied his horse off and they went inside.

A short, portly man who looked more like the clerk in a general store than an undertaker turned and looked at them.

"El jefe," he said, staring at James curiously.

"Deputy James Shaye," Montoya said, "this is Ignacio Benedicto de la Vega, our undertaker."

"Señor," de la Vega said, cautiously.

"And in the absence of a proper doctor, he does his best," Montoya said.

Montoya then spoke to the undertaker in rapid Spanish that James could not follow.

Then he said to James, "Please, follow us."

The two men led James through a curtained doorway, down a hall, past two rooms that held coffins in various stages of construction, to a back room he could only assume was for coffins already completed, and possibly holding a body.

He licked his lips as they opened the door.

Instead of a coffin he saw a bed, with a man on it, bandaged around his midriff.

"Hello, little brother," Thomas said.

"You're supposed to be dead," James said.

With a wry grin Thomas said, "Sorry to disappoint you."

The sheriff and undertaker left the two brothers alone. Thomas sat on the bed, while James sat on the straight-backed wooden chair in the room, and they caught up.

"They came at me in the street," Thomas explained. "It was my own fault, though. I knew at least one of them was watchin' me. I was careless. Pa's gonna kill me."

"He'll be glad to get the chance," James pointed out.

"They started firin' from opposite sides of the street, gettin' me in a crossfire while I was in the middle of the street, crossin' over. I got hit in the first volley, and then it got confusin'."

He shifted, getting more comfortable on the bed.

"People started running this way and that.

I fired back, but soon lost sight of them, and then suddenly the sheriff was there — and I went out.

"I gotta give Montoya credit. He thought fast, convinced everybody I was dead, then had some men carry me here to the undertaker's. They're old friends, and Ignacio was willin' to help. Montoya had him patch me up, stop the bleedin', and then they left me back here to rest."

"And the Flemings?"

"They left town, thinkin' they'd got the job done."

"But how are you?" James asked.

"The bullet took out a big chunk of skin," Thomas explained, "but kept goin'. Ignacio stopped the bleeding and then wrapped me up tight. So nobody knows I'm alive but the sheriff, the undertaker, and now you."

"What was your plan?"

"I figured to rest up a couple of days, and then start trackin' them again."

"Alone?"

"Well," Thomas said, "I did figure you'd be along, eventually. I thought Candy had to be plannin' to join up with them, and he'd lead you right here. What happened to him?"

"He's dead."

"How?"

208

"He tried to kill me in my room in Tubac, but I heard him comin'."

"Tubac. So you met Irma."

"I did, and her bartender. She gave me some food, and a room —"

"And offered to warm your bed for a price."

"She did. I turned her down."

"Hey," Thomas said, "I turned her down, too. This has been all business, James."

"Well," James said, "after I got to my room, he tied and gagged Irma and the bartender and left them in the kitchen. Then he came for me."

"Are they okay?"

"They're fine," James said. "After I killed Candy, I untied them. Irma wants us to come back that way."

"She would. She's a good cook, though."

"Oh, and Belle wants us to come back, too."

"You met Belle?"

"She's the one who told me you're still alive. She heard it from someone over here.

"Why'd she do that?"

"She's hopin' we'll come back and get rid of Adam Grey."

"Grey, the gambler," Thomas said. "You met him, too."

"Sheriff Dewey warned me about him,"

James said, "and he said I could trust Montoya about as much as I trusted him."

"Which you'd think ain't much, but Montoya really came through for me. Guess when it came right down to it, the badge was more important."

"Same with Dewey," James said. "He'd also like Grey gone."

"Because he owes him money."

"And so does Belle," James said, "so maybe they're only lookin' out for their own interests, but it's managed to help us."

Thomas put his hand on his brother's shoulder and said, "It sure did. When you heard I was dead, you didn't happen to send a telegram to Pa, did you?"

"No," James said, "I knew you weren't dead."

"How'd you know that?"

"You're just too ornery to let the Fleming brothers kill you."

"Well," Thomas said, "now we're gonna go after them together. Brothers against brothers."

"But you ain't fit to ride."

"As long as I'm wrapped up tight I can ride," Thomas said. "We can't let them get too far ahead of us."

"Which way did they go?" James asked.

"South, farther into Mexico. It could be

they're still aimin' to meet up with other gang members."

"It sure would be good if we could catch up to them long before that," James pointed out.

"I agree with you there, little brother," Thomas said. "You got a room yet?"

"No," James said, "I wanted to check on you first."

"Why don't you check into a hotel, get some food, and then maybe bring me back somethin'," Thomas said. "I'm starvin'."

"Haven't they been feedin' you?"

"I've only been here since yesterday," Thomas said. "We haven't gotten the kinks worked out yet, like which one of them is gonna bring me food."

"So now it's my job," James said.

Thomas laughed. "You got that right, little brother."

THIRTY-SEVEN

Dan Shaye released his three prisoners the next morning, and they immediately mounted up and rode out of town. If they were, indeed, in league with Cole Doucette, they'd be passing the word on to him that Tate Kingdom was in town, and backing the sheriff's play. If not . . . no harm, no foul.

Kingdom spent the next two days relaxing in the saloon, playing poker, pausing only to go out and have meals, then returning to his seat at the table, which was held for him. It was not a big money game, not quite penny ante. It was just meant to pass the time.

Shaye spent his time continuing to worry about his sons and conduct twice as many rounds around town as he needed to, also to pass the time. The mayor'd had no further word on the location of Cole Doucette, so they were still adopting a wait-and-see attitude.

Finally, three days after he released the three prisoners, nine men rode into town, and at the head of the column was one Cole Doucette . . .

Shaye had been sitting outside in front of his office when they rode in. He watched as they passed him on the way to the livery. Doucette never looked at him once.

He knew it was Doucette because Mayor Snow came running into his office minutes later, in a panic, shouting, "He's here! Cole Doucette is here!"

"I saw him," Shaye said calmly.

"Well, whataya gonna do about it, Sheriff?" the Mayor demanded.

"I'm not gonna do anythin' rash, Mayor, without considerin' my options."

"Your options?" Snow exploded. "Arrest him!"

"And the seven men with him?" Shaye asked. "For what?"

"For . . . for . . . for . . . Seven? I heard he had five."

"Somebody miscounted," Shaye said. "Eight men rode in with him."

"Eight." Snow covered his face with his hands. "They could burn down the whole town."

"But Doucette is here for you, Mayor," Shaye said, "not the town. Why don't you just give yourself up?"

Snow dropped his hands and gaped at Shaye. "He'll kill me!"

"But the town would be safe," Shaye said. "Isn't that your first priority?"

Mayor Snow pointed a thick index finger at Shaye.

"Don't get smart, Dan!" he shouted. "It's your responsibility to protect me and the town. I expect you to do your job."

"Well then, Mayor," Shaye said, "get out of my office and let me do it."

"And it better be soon!" Snow finished, his voice cracking.

He walked to the door, opened it about a foot, peered out, and then carefully stepped through it.

Shaye waited a few minutes, then stepped out himself and sat back down. He wanted to watch and see where Doucette and his men went next.

Cole Doucette and his men dismounted at the livery stable.

"Did you see the lawman, Cole?" Sam Hawko asked.

"I saw him."

"That was Dan Shaye."

"The man who ran you and Tayback out of town."

"He didn't run us!" Tayback complained.

"What would you call it?" Doucette asked.

"Well, I'd say —"

"Never mind," Doucette said. "Just get these horses taken care of. I'm goin' to a hotel."

"What about the rest of us?" Paul Tayback asked.

"Find places of your own," Doucette said, "but stay where I can find you. That means no cathouse, you understand? All of you?"

The other seven men nodded their understanding.

"And when you go to the saloon, remember, one beer each. Hawko, you see to it."

"I will, boss."

"Nils," Doucette said, "you're with me."

Nils the Swede nodded and followed Doucette out of the livery. He was a very big, blond man, like most Swedes.

Doucette and Nils walked to the center of town, to the hotel they had passed on the way in. Along the way they also had to pass the sheriff's office again. Doucette saw Shaye sitting in front, but made as if he didn't.

"We goin' to the hotel, boss?"

"That's right, Nils."

215

"Why can't we get a drink first?"

"No drinks for you, Nils," Doucette said. "Not till we do what we came to do."

"Why not?"

"Because you get crazy when you drink," Doucette said. "I'll let you know when I want you to get crazy. Understand?"

"Yes, boss," Nils said. "I understand."

"I'm gonna get you a room next to mine, so you'll be close at hand. If you hear anythin', you come a runnin'."

"Yes, sir."

"Let's go."

Doucette and Nils went inside the hotel.

Shaye watched as Doucette and a big, blond man walked back down the street from the livery. He'd expected them to go to the saloon first, but maybe that's what the other men would do.

He thought about waiting for them in the saloon, then considered going to the hotel to talk to Doucette when he didn't have all the other men around him.

Then he got another idea.

"You want me to what?" Mayor Snow demanded.

"Talk to Doucette."

"You're crazy."

They were in Snow's office, where Shaye had found the man sitting behind his desk, wringing his hands.

"I'll go with you," Shaye said. "He's at the hotel, gettin' a room. We'll have to move fast, while he doesn't have his men around him."

"I still say you're — oh, wait. While I'm talkin' to him you're gonna kill him, right?"

"No, I'm not," Shaye said. "I'm gonna try to reason with him."

"And if you can't? Then will you kill him?"

"I'll warn him."

"So when will you kill him?" Snow asked.

"When he tries to kill me, I suppose."

"Well, that'll happen," Snow said. "You'll see."

"Come on, Snow," Shaye said. "Let's go and talk to the man. Maybe he ain't here for you at all."

Snow stood up, but said, "This is a mistake."

"Maybe," Shaye said. "Let's find out just how big a mistake it might be."

THIRTY-EIGHT

Shaye found out from the desk clerk which room Cole Doucette had been put in.

As he and Mayor Snow walked down the hall Snow said, "I still think you should just shoot him when he opens the door."

"Not gonna do that, Mayor," Shaye said. Very quickly he reached into the mayor's jacket and pulled out a small .32. "And neither are you."

"Hey!"

"Just relax," Shaye said, "and let me do the talkin'." He tucked Snow's .32 into his belt, then knocked on Doucette's door.

The door was opened immediately, and Cole Doucette stood there with his gun in his hand. He was over six feet tall, thick from the years he'd spent in prison. He was probably younger than he looked, which was about fifty. Men aged in prison.

"Sheriff Shaye, ain't it?" he asked.

"That's right."

"And Mayor Snow," Doucette said. "Nice to see you again, Mayor. Only you weren't a mayor when I saw you last. Just a district attorney, puttin' me away."

"For somethin' you did," the mayor said.

"For protectin' myself," Doucette ordered.

"You wanna put up that gun?" Shaye asked. "We came here to talk."

"That right?" Doucette holstered his gun. "Then by all means, come on in. Let's talk."

He backed up and allowed them to enter. The mayor came in last and left the door open. Shaye figured he wanted a quick way out if things went wrong.

"What brings you here, Sheriff?" Doucette asked.

"That's what I want to ask you, Mr. Doucette," Shaye said. "What brings you to Vengeance Creek?"

" 'Mr. Doucette'?" he asked. "You know how long it's been since I was called that?"

"You did your time," Shaye said. "You deserve the respect."

"That right, Mr. Mayor?" Doucette asked. "You think I deserve respect?"

"I guess that depends," Snow said.

"On what I want, right?"

"That's right."

Doucette walked to the bed and sat down. "Vengeance Creek," Doucette said. "This

219

town's got a fittin' name. When I got out of prison, all I wanted was vengeance."

"And now?" Shaye asked.

"Now I'm not sure," Doucette said.

"Then why'd you come?" Snow asked.

"I was on my way here," the man said, with a shrug. "I thought, why not finish the trip?"

"With seven men?" Shaye asked.

"I'm used to ridin' with men to watch my back," Doucette said.

"So . . . you're not here to kill me?" Snow asked.

"Kill you?" Doucette asked. He pretended to think about it. "I admit while I was in prison I thought about killin' you. Dreamed about it, even. But once I got out, and headed here . . . I realized somethin'."

"What's that?" Shaye asked.

"I don't wanna go back to prison," Doucette said, "and killin' you, Mr. Mayor, would send me right back there." He nodded at Shaye. "The sheriff here would see to that."

Snow looked at Shaye, then back at Doucette.

"I hope I can believe you, Dou— Mr. Doucette," the mayor said.

"You don't have to believe me, Mr. Mayor," Doucette said. "Just wait and see."

220

He smiled.

The mayor, still nervous, said, "Okay, Dan, I guess we got what we wanted."

"I guess so, Mayor." Shaye looked at Doucette. "Thanks for talkin' to us, Mr. Doucette."

"My pleasure, gents, my pleasure," Doucette said. "Say, where's the best place in town to get a steak?"

Outside the hotel the mayor said, "I need a drink. You want a drink, Dan?"

"Sure, why not?"

They crossed over to the Renegade Saloon and went inside. The mayor had a regular table that was always left open for him, so they went to it. One of the pretty young saloon girls took their order and brought them each a beer.

"Thanks, Gina," Snow said.

"Sure, Mr. Mayor, honey."

They each sipped, and then Snow sat back, looking visibly relieved.

"What did you think?" he asked.

"Of what?" Shaye asked.

"Of what Doucette said, of course," Mayor Snow said.

"Oh," Shaye said, "he's here to kill you, all right."

Mayor Snow put his mug down with a

221

bang. "What?"

"I didn't believe a word he said, Mayor," Shaye said. "He's here to kill you. It's just a matter of when he'll try."

"Well . . . Jesus!" The mayor picked up his beer and drank it straight down.

THIRTY-NINE

Dan Shaye was dead sure Cole Doucette and his men were in Vengeance Creek to cause havoc. What he was also dead sure of was that it would not be at a time of their choosing.

Since Doucette was choosing to play it as if he had decided not to kill Mayor Snow, Shaye knew he had some time to whittle down Doucette's force of eight men. But he'd need help.

He still didn't know if Doucette was aware that Tate Kingdom was in town, or that Kingdom had helped Shaye. But Kingdom was the only person in town Shaye knew he could go to. There might have been some citizens who were willing to pick up a gun, but he doubted it.

He also knew Kingdom spent his time at the poker table in the Renegade Saloon, so after Mayor Snow went home to hide in his bedroom, Shaye went to the saloon. It was afternoon, the place was not doing its usual evening business, so it was quiet enough for him to hear the sound of poker chips as they clattered into the pot.

He walked to the bar and told the bartender, "Let me have a beer."

"Sure, Sheriff."

Once he had the beer, he turned and watched the game. For all intents and purposes, Kingdom was concentrating on the cards, but Shaye knew the gunman was immediately aware of him as he walked in.

He sipped his beer, watched the game, and as Kingdom was raking in a pot, he moved.

"Come on, Kingdom," he said, as he reached the table, "we need to talk."

Kingdom sat back. "What's on your mind, Sheriff?"

"I had some complaints about you."

"Complaints?" Kingdom asked. "I haven't left this table except to eat and sleep."

"He's right, Sheriff," one of the players said. "He's been takin' our money for days."

"Shut up, Munski," Shaye said. "This doesn't concern you. Kingdom? You comin'? Or do I have to take your gun?"

Kingdom finally got the message.

"No, no, Sheriff, that's okay," he said, pushing his chair back. "I'll come along

224

quietly."

As he reached to drag his chips into his hat Shaye said, "Leave 'em. They'll be here when you get back."

"You think so?" Kingdom asked.

"I know so." Shaye looked at each of the other players in turn. "They'll be here when he gets back, right?"

"Right, Sheriff," Munski said, "right."

"They'll be here," one of the other players said.

"So where we goin', Sheriff?" Kingdom asked.

"My office," Shaye said. "Just follow me and shut up."

The two men walked out of the saloon together.

"Trouble, Sheriff?" Kingdom asked.

"Cole Doucette's in town."

"Oh."

"With seven men."

"Oh," Kingdom said, in a different tone.

"I have an idea, but I need your help."

"Well," Kingdom replied, "like I said, all I've been doing is playing poker. Frankly, my ass is starting to hurt from sitting so long."

"Good," Shaye said, "because what I have in mind doesn't involve much sitting."

"Care to give me a hint?" the gunman asked.

"Yeah," Shaye said, "when we get to my office."

From the window of his room, Cole Doucette watched Sheriff Shaye and another man cross the street and enter the sheriff's office.

"Nils!"

The big Swede came over to the window.

"Yah, boss?"

"The sheriff just went into his office with another man," Doucette said. "Find Hawko and tell him I wanna know who it is."

"I can find out, boss."

"You're too noticeable," Doucette said. "Just do what I ask you to do, Nils."

"Sure, boss."

Doucette went back to looking out the window, wondering if the sheriff and the mayor believed anything he'd been saying to them. Probably not the sheriff. He was too smart. He was going to have to be taken care of before Doucette could get to the mayor. He'd spent too many hours in prison planning this for anything to go wrong.

"How do you want to handle this?" Kingdom asked, taking a seat in front of Shaye's desk.

Shaye poured two cups of coffee from the office pot and handed Kingdom one, then sat at his desk.

"We had a talk with Doucette. He claims he's not here to kill Mayor Snow, that he changed his mind. I think he's settin' us up, but he's probably not gonna act for a while."

"Which means?"

"Which means the seven men he brought with him have time to get themselves in trouble and end up in my jail."

"Or in the ground," Kingdom said.

"I'd prefer not, but if it comes to that . . ."

"So what do you want me to do?"

"Just back my play, whatever it turns out to be," Shaye said. "Like you did last time. You didn't even have to draw your gun."

"Maybe we'll get lucky and it'll stay that way," Kingdom commented.

"I don't know," Shaye said. "Doucette did a lot of time, thanks to our good mayor. I don't think he's about to forget it."

"So where's the mayor?"

"Hidin' in his house or his office," Shaye said.

"And Doucette's men?"

"All I know is, they weren't in his room with him," Shaye said.

227

"This town have a whorehouse?"

"One," Shaye said. "You mean you haven't been there?"

"I don't like whores very much," Kingdom said. "But his men might."

"They have to be somewhere," Shaye said. "Hotels, whorehouse, maybe some saloons."

"And wherever they are, you think they're going to get into trouble."

Shaye put his coffee cup down and said, "I can practically guarantee it."

FORTY

Two days after James arrived in Nogales, Mexico, he and his brother, Thomas, stepped out of the undertaker's office and onto the street.

"You okay?" James asked.

"I told you yesterday I was okay," Thomas said.

Their horses, brought there earlier by James, were tied to a hitching post.

"Time to ride out, then," James said.

Thomas nodded. "Let's do it."

They mounted their horses and started riding out of town. Before they could leave, however, Sheriff Montoya stepped into their path.

"Sheriff," Thomas said. "Glad to see you. I wanted to thank you for savin' my bacon."

"Don't know if you will still be thanking me, *señor,*" Montoya said.

"Why's that?"

"I just heard that the Fleming brothers

have joined up with the rest of their gang."

"And you want to tell us where?" James asked.

"I want to warn you," Montoya said. "Perhaps you will go back to the United States, back to your Vengeance Creek, while you still can."

"Afraid we can't do that, Sheriff," Thomas said. "We've still got a job to do."

"I cannot talk you out of it?" Montoya asked.

" 'Fraid not," James said, "so you should probably just tell us what you know."

Montoya took a deep breath, then gave a fatalistic shrug of his shoulders. The two crazy *gringos* were not to be dissuaded.

"Two days to the south is a town called San Lupita," he said. "The Flemings and their gang are there now."

"And where are they headed from there?" Thomas asked.

"That I do not know, *señor*," the sheriff said. "My information is limited."

The Shayes wondered if the sheriff's limited information was also reliable.

"Two days south," James asked, "at what rate of travel?"

"Ah, that is a good question, *señor*," Montoya said. "Perhaps it is two days at a true Mexican rate of travel. Two young *gringos* like you, with good horses, perhaps a day."

The two brothers exchanged a glance.

"Directly south?" James asked.

"Directly south, *señor*," Montoya said.

"Thank you, Sheriff Montoya."

"Vaya con dios, mis amigos."

They rode out of Nogales and headed south.

"Do you think this is reliable information?" James asked several minutes later.

"He did save my life," Thomas pointed out, "so I guess we should take it at face value. Besides, what else have we got?"

"I guess we better ride then — at our *gringo* rate of travel."

Thomas laughed as they spurred their horses into a gallop.

The Shaye brothers reached San Lupita that night after dark. They considered camping outside of town when darkness fell, but were able to see some lights in the distance, so decided to push on. They rode more slowly, so as not to risk injury to the horses.

San Lupita was a small town. The lights were coming from only a few of the buildings, including a cantina with EL DIABLO ROJO above the doorway.

They reined in their horses in front of the

cantina and dismounted.

"How many of the gang do you think would recognize us?" James asked.

"Well, the brothers for sure. With the others, it would depend on how much attention they were paying that day in the Renegade."

James frowned. "Now I wish I'd paid more attention myself. I don't know if I'd recognize any of *them.*"

"We'll recognize them," Thomas said, "if they go for their guns."

They went inside the cantina. They didn't know if it was the time of night, or if the place was always that empty. The light was bright inside, though, and the bartender smiled as they approached the bar.

"What is your pleasure, *señores*?" he asked.

"*Dos cervezas,*" Thomas said.

As the bartender fetched their beers, James asked, "How big is your town? In the dark it's hard to tell."

"We are small, *señor,*" the man said, setting their beers down on the bar.

"We saw the lights from a distance," Thomas said, "but didn't know if it was a town or just a house."

"We are a town, *señor,*" the barman said,

but he spread his arms and added, "but just barely."

Thomas and James had decided ahead of time to play it straight. There was no time for games anymore.

"We were told that some men we're lookin' for might be here," Thomas said.

"Men, *señor*?"

"*Gringos,* like us," James said. "We're lookin' to join up with them."

The bartender studied the two of them for a moment before answering.

"There were some men here, *señor,*" he said, finally. "First two, and then four arrived."

"Are they still here?"

"They ate, they drank," the man said, "they used our women, and then they left."

"Did they hurt anybody?"

"Perhaps they were a little too rough with our *putas,*" the man said, "but that is what they get paid for, eh?"

"The *putas,*" Thomas said, "the whores, are they . . . available?"

"*Si, señor,*" the bartender said. "They are in the back rooms. You would like, perhaps, one each?"

"No," James said, "just one will do."

"For the two of you?" The man looked surprised.

Thomas took out some money. "We can pay."

"Well, *señor,*" he said, "as long as you can pay . . . go through that doorway to room *dos* — two — and knock. Elena will let you in." He shrugged. "Then you can tell her what you want."

"And who do we pay?" James asked.

"You pay her, *señor,*" the man said. "She will be the one doing the work, no?"

"Yes," Thomas said. "Thanks."

James started to leave the bar, but Thomas put his hand on his brother's arm. "Finish your beer. She's not goin' anywhere."

"Right," James said, "right."

"And when we get back there," Thomas said, "why don't I do the talkin', little brother?"

"Why?"

"Well, you do get a little tongue-tied around a certain kind of woman."

"I'll be fine!" James groused. "Just fine."

FORTY-ONE

They finished their beers, then walked to the doorway at the back of the room and went down a hallway to room two. Thomas knocked, and when the door opened, both brothers had to stare. Thomas thought he heard his brother's jaw drop. The Mexican woman was all wild black hair, black eyes, and a body barely covered by a peasant blouse and skirt. She also had a bruise on her face, probably from the rough treatment the bartender had mentioned. James stared at her bare legs, then averted his eyes.

"*Señores?*" she said.

"The bartender said that you, uh, work here as a . . ." James trailed off.

"My brother's tryin' to say we'd like to pay you for some information."

"Information?" She put her hands on her hips and stared at them in surprise. "That is all you want from me?"

"That's it," Thomas said.

"Then come in, come in, *señores,*" she said. When they were inside she asked, "And for this information would you like my clothes on or off?"

"Oh," James said. "Uh, don't do that. You can, uh, leave your clothes on. We just wanna talk."

"I do not have any chairs for you to sit in," she said, waving her arms. "I have only the bed." In waving, the blouse fell further down her shoulders, causing James to look away again.

"Are you all right?" she asked him.

"He's fine," Thomas said. "Just a little shy."

"That is sweet," she said. "I could help him with his shyness, *señor.* I am very experienced."

The girl looked to Thomas like she was a year or two younger than James, not older. But he knew for a fact she was more experienced than either one of them.

"That's okay," Thomas said. "Look, we have questions about some men who were here."

"Ah, the *gringo bandidos*?"

"How do you know they were *bandidos*?" Thomas asked.

"As I said, *señor,*" she replied, sitting on the bed, "I am very experienced. They were *bandidos.* There is no doubt about that."

"Well, we're lawmen from the United States," Thomas said, "and we're huntin' those men. Did they say anything about where they were goin' when they left here?"

"Left here?" she asked.

"Yes," Thomas said. "When they were, uh, done with you, where did they go?"

"But *señor,*" she said, "they did not go anywhere."

"Are you sayin' they're still here?" James asked.

"*Si, señor.*"

"But . . . where?"

She stood up, spread her arms and said, "Here."

Thomas and James looked at each other.

"They have rooms here?" Thomas asked.

"*Si, señor.*"

"But . . . the bartender didn't tell us that," Thomas said.

"Of course not, *señor,*" she said. "They are paying him a lot of money."

"Great," Thomas said.

"So now we're trapped in here?" James asked.

"*Señorita,* your name is Elena, right?" Thomas asked.

"*Si, señor.*"

"Why are you tellin' us this?" Thomas

asked. "Won't the bartender be mad at you?"

"I do not care if he is angry," she said. "He does nothing to protect us from these *bandidos*. Pigs!" She practically spat the word out.

"Us?" James asked.

"*Si, mi hermana,* my sister, Isabella."

"And where is she?"

"Down the hall, in her room."

"Alone?"

"Probably not," Elena said.

"How many rooms are here?" Thomas asked.

"Six."

"Yours, Isabella's, and four others. Are the *bandidos* in those?"

"*Si,* they are sharing."

"Two of them are brothers," James said. "Are they in the same room?"

"*Si.*"

James looked at Thomas. "What do you think? Do they know we're here?"

"Only if the bartender told them," Thomas said.

"If he had, wouldn't they be in here by now?" James asked.

"You'd think so," Thomas said. "He must have known Elena would tell us they're here."

"So what's his game?" James asked.

"He is a greedy man," Elena said, "a very greedy man."

"If that's the case," Thomas said, "then maybe he wants to see if we'll offer him more money than the Flemings did." He looked at Elena. "Is there any law here?"

"*El jefe?* No, *señor*. No law."

Thomas looked at James. "So we're on our own."

"We should talk to the bartender," James said. "If he hasn't told them we're here yet, we can surprise them."

"Yeah," Thomas said, "but we better move quietly."

As Thomas turned, Elena suddenly grabbed his arm.

"If my sister is with them . . ."

"Don't worry," Thomas said. "We'll do our best to see that you and your sister are not harmed."

"*Gracias,*" she said. She released his arm, then reached past him and touched James's cheek, making him blush.

"*Tan dulce,*" she said.

FORTY-TWO

Thomas opened the door, peered out and saw that the hall was deserted. He stepped out and beckoned James to follow him. They closed Elena's door, stopped to listen, but didn't hear anything from the other rooms.

They went back along the hall to the cantina. The bartender — Elena said Maximilian — "Max" — was his name — was still slouched behind the bar. When he saw the two lawmen, he perked up.

"More beers, *señores*?"

"Sure, Max," Thomas said, "why not?"

He happily set two more beers on the bar for them and took their money.

"Max, Elena told us about the guests in your other rooms," James said.

"*Si, señor.*" Max held his forefinger to his lips. "They are asleep."

"So you haven't told them that we're here," Thomas said.

"No, *señor,*" Max said, then added, "not yet."

"What makes you think we just won't kill you to keep you quiet?" Thomas asked.

"*Señores,*" Max said, with a smile, "you are *gringo* lawmen. A Mexican lawman, he would shoot me right between the eyes without hesitation. But not a *gringo* lawman. You are much too . . . how do you say . . . moral?"

"So if we pay you more than they paid you, you'll keep quiet," James said.

"*Si, señor,*" Max said with a shrug. "I am a simple businessman."

"And you're not afraid they'll kill you when they find out?" James asked.

"*Señor,*" the barman said, "I am not afraid of *bandidos,* or *federales.* If I die, what do I lose? This place?" He shrugged. "God will decide when it is my time. What I do in the meantime has no effect on the outcome. Do you see?"

"Yeah," Thomas said, "I see."

"I don't," James said. "You mean you're gonna die when you die, and what you do until then doesn't matter?"

"Exactly, *señor.*"

James looked at Thomas and at Max. "Well, that ain't right. What we do has gotta matter somewhere along the line."

241

"If that is what you believe, *señor* . . ." Max said, with another shrug.

"But —" James started, only to be cut off by his brother.

"What any of us believes don't matter now," he said. "We can talk about it another time. Max, how much do you want to just keep quiet and let us do what we came here to do?"

"Two hundred American dollars."

"We don't have two hundred dollars!" James snapped.

"That is unfortunate, *señor.* The *bandidos* you seek paid me one hundred dollars to wake them if anyone . . . suspicious rode in."

"I tell you what," Thomas said. "There's a reward due on each one of them. Once we've captured them, you'll be entitled to it all."

Max rubbed his jaw. "That is very interesting, *señor.* American rewards can be very much money."

"Yes, they can."

"But what if you do not capture them?"

"Then you'll have their hundred dollars."

"Which they will want back if I have not warned them about you."

"I thought you weren't afraid of *bandidos*?" James asked.

242

"That is true, *señor*," Max said, "but I am also not a stupid man."

"We should be able to come to some kind of understandin', Max," Thomas said.

"I understand money, *señor*."

"Yeah," Thomas said, "we all do."

FORTY-THREE

Thomas and James gave Max, the bartender, all the money they had on them — which came to forty-three dollars — and promised much more from the rewards that would be due for the outlaws.

"And I can keep the hundred American dollars they gave me?" he asked.

"Yes," Thomas said, "you can keep it."

So now the brothers had to figure out how to take the six men who were in the cantina's rooms, especially if some of them were with Elena's sister, Isabella.

"Max, do you know if Isabella is alone in her room?" Thomas asked.

"I do not know this, *señor,*" Max admitted.

"Can you find out?"

Max shrugged. "I can knock on her door, but if she is not alone I will wake the man with her."

Thomas looked at James. "Once he wakes

up, he might want to come out for a drink or a piss."

"That might not be a bad idea," James pointed out. "Then we could take at least one of them without the others knowing."

"Or two," Max said.

Both brothers looked at him.

"If she is with two men," Max added.

"We can still handle two," Thomas said.

"One each," James agreed.

"What about it?" Thomas asked Max. "Will you go back and see?"

"Since you're not scared, and all," James added.

"I will go," Max said, "for you, *señores.*"

He poured himself a shot glass of tequila, downed it, wiped his mouth with the back of his hand, and came out from behind the bar.

"Now remember," Thomas said, "just knock loud enough for them to hear you in the room — not loud enough for everyone to hear you."

"And what if they are light sleepers, *señor?*" Max asked.

"We'll just deal with that if it happens," Thomas said.

Max went to the doorway, then started up the hall. Thomas and James remained in the cantina, just outside the hall, to watch. They were ready to draw their guns if the need arose.

"How's your side?" James asked, in a low voice.

"What?"

"Your wound," James said. "How is it?"

"You're askin' me that now?"

"I didn't have time before," James said. "I mean, we rode a long way. I'm just wonderin' —"

"My side it fine, James!" Thomas said. "Let's concentrate on what we're doin' here."

"Okay, okay," James said.

Max had reached the door to Isabella's room. He turned to indicate this to Thomas and James by pointing at it.

Thomas nodded and waved at him to go on and do what he was supposed to do.

The bartender listened at the door first, then proceeded to knock on it very lightly.

They all waited. Max was about to knock again when the door opened. Thomas and James couldn't see who had opened it, but Max and that person talked very briefly, and then the bartender came back down the hall.

"Poor Isabella," he said.

"Why poor Isabella?" James asked.

"They have been very abusive to her, *señore*s."

"Why her more than Elena?" James asked.

"I do not know," Max said. "Perhaps because she is younger, and smaller."

"She's younger than Elena?" James asked.

"Okay, never mind that!" Thomas snapped, fighting to keep his voice low. "How many men are in there with her?"

"One."

"Did he wake up when you knocked?"

"He perhaps stirred," Max said, "but I do not know if he woke."

"What did you say to Isabella?" Thomas asked.

"I said I was checking to see if she was all right," Max said, "and I asked who was in the room with her."

"Is it one of the Fleming brothers?" Thomas asked.

"No, *señor,* one of their men."

Thomas looked at James.

"What do we do now?" James asked.

"Let's give it a few minutes and see what happens," Thomas said. "If he comes out, we'll take him."

"And if he doesn't?"

"Then we have to figure out a way to take them all," Thomas said.

They all moved quietly back to the bar, where Thomas and James still had mugs of beer waiting. Max poured himself another glass of tequila.

"What are the chances of someone else comin' in tonight?" Thomas asked.

"I would say slim, *señor,* but . . ."

"But what?" James asked.

"I did not expect the two of you." He shrugged helplessly.

"Okay," Thomas said, "let's assume nobody else comes in tonight."

"And?" James asked.

"That gives us time to come up with a plan."

"You know what Pa always says," James said.

"What does he say, *señor*?" Max asked. "Your *papa*?"

"If you don't have a plan goin' in," James replied, "you better have one comin' out."

They all thought about that, and then Max said, "He is a very wise man, your *papa.*"

FORTY-FOUR

"So what's our plan?" James asked.

"Well," Thomas said, "for one thing we gotta stop drinkin' beer. We'll end up too drunk to shoot straight."

They both drained their mugs and pushed the empties toward Max, who took them away.

"And second?" James asked.

"I'm still workin' on second."

"Why don't we just go into their rooms one at a time and take 'em?" James asked.

"That'd work as long as nobody wakes up and sounds the alarm," Thomas said. "We could also wait for them all to come out for breakfast in the morning, and get the drop on them in this room."

"They're on the run," James said. "They'll be wearin' their guns. In bed, the best they've got is their guns close by, or on the bedpost in their gunbelts."

"Good point, little brother," Thomas said.

"Okay, let's go room by room, starting with Isabella's."

Thomas and James approached the doorway to the hall and looked at each other.

"Quietly, little brother," Thomas said.

James nodded, and they stepped into the narrow hallway.

From behind they heard Max come to the door. They thought he was interested in watching, but in the next moment his voice boomed, *"Los Asesinos! Los Asesinos estan aqui!"*

In shock, James turned to look at the bartender. Thomas was looking ahead as the doors opened and the outlaws came running out, guns in their hands. He reached out to push James to one side while he squeezed himself against the other wall, putting as much space between them as he could.

And then the small, enclosed space exploded in a rain of gunfire.

Thomas fired, trying to be as accurate as he could with each shot. Next to him he could hear his brother firing as well. Lead whizzed past them as the outlaws also fired, the sound deafening in the hallway. Thomas heard cries of pain and anguish, and then the sound of gun hammers falling on empty chambers.

And then it was over, in what seemed like hours but was actually seconds.

Thomas looked at James. "Are you all right? Are you hit?"

James looked down at himself, actually patting his chest and stomach.

"I-I don't seem to be." He looked at Thomas. "What about you. Is that blood?"

Thomas looked down, saw the blood on his shirt, patted himself the way his brother had done.

"That's the old wound," Thomas said. "I haven't been hit again."

"In this hall," James said, "how is it possible neither one of us was hit?"

"I don't know," Thomas said. They looked at the outlaws, saw the bodies on the floor. "They weren't so lucky."

They walked to the fallen *bandidos* and checked each one.

"Dead," Thomas said.

"Here, too," James said.

When they were through, they realized there were four bodies.

"The Fleming boys ain't here," Thomas said.

Two doors opened, and Elena and a small girl who was obviously her sister, Isabella, peered out.

"Es seguro?" Isabella asked.

251

"Is it safe?" Elena translated.

"Just a minute," Thomas said.

There was only one closed door. Thomas and James reloaded and walked to it. As Thomas nodded, they slammed it open and burst into the room, guns ready. All they found was an empty interior and an open window.

"Sonofabitch!" Thomas said. "They let their gang engage us and lit out."

"Damn it!" James swore.

They walked back out into the hall and told the two girls, "It's safe."

The sisters came out and embraced each other.

Thomas and James walked to the end of the hall and found Max lying there, riddled with bullets.

"Jesus," James said, "it looks like every shot they fired hit him."

"And not us," Thomas said, holstering his gun. "I think that, at least, calls for a drink."

"Shouldn't we go after Red and Harry?"

"In the dark?" Thomas asked. "We'll kill ourselves or the horses."

They walked to the bar. Thomas got behind it and drew two beers.

"You think they'll keep goin' south?" James asked.

"Why would they head back to the border?" Thomas asked. "They've got to lie low for a while, and there's no better place for that than Mexico."

The two girls came out, still with their arms around each other, and looked down at the dead bartender.

"We're sorry," Thomas said, starting to apologize for Max getting killed, "but he —"

They both interrupted him by spitting on Max's lifeless body.

"Never mind," Thomas said.

FORTY-FIVE

Dan Shaye finally decided that the one place Doucette and his men could not avoid forever was the Renegade Saloon.

The next day he managed to locate most of Doucette's men. Three of them got rooms in a local rooming house, while the other three found lodging in various hotels. The only one in the same hotel as Doucette was a big Swede named Nils.

Two of Doucette's men made it easy. They went into the Renegade, got into a poker game — not with Kingdom — and then got into a fight with some of the other players. Shaye, who had been on the lookout for trouble, immediately got the drop on them and took them into custody.

"You can't put us in here for fightin'!" one of them shouted as he locked their cells.

"Fightin's against the law in this county," Shaye told them.

"How long we gonna be in here?" the

other one asked.

"That depends," Shaye said, but he didn't bother telling them on what. He went out and closed the cell block door, even while they were still hollerin'.

Mayor Snow rushed into the sheriff's office. Shaye was surprised to see the man outside his house or his own office.

"What's on your mind, Mayor?"

"Is that your plan?" Snow asked. "Lock up Doucette's men. That still leaves him free to kill me."

"I thought you believed him when he told you that he didn't want to kill you?"

"Well, no," Snow groused, "you talked me out of that."

"Then why ain't you home where it's safe?"

The mayor drew himself up to his full medium height and said, "I can't hide forever. What kind of message does that send to the town about their mayor?"

"That he's smart?"

"That he's a coward!" the mayor snapped. "I may *be* a coward, but I don't want the townspeople knowing that."

"Mayor," Shaye said, "it ain't cowardly to know your limitations. You're on watch for Doucette if he comes after you. Therefore, the best thing for you to do is to stay outta sight."

"You think so?"

"I know so."

"Well," the mayor said, "since it's your idea, Sheriff, I'll do that. I'll stay out of sight. If you need me, I'll either be at my house, or city hall."

"Okay," Shaye said, "if I need you, that's where I'll look."

As the mayor opened the door to go out, Tate Kingdom appeared. The gunman allowed the mayor to leave, the two men looking each other over, and then entered himself.

"Who's that?" Kingdom asked.

"That's our illustrious mayor."

"He's what this is all about?"

"He is," Shaye said. "What are you doin' here?"

"I was takin' a break from my game and heard you nabbed two of Doucette's men."

"I did," Shaye said. "They're in cells."

"Sorry I wasn't there for back-up."

"That's okay," Shaye said. "I was able to handle two."

"What do you think Doucette will do when he hears?"

"He might come and have a talk," Shaye said, "but there ain't much he can do, un-

256

less he and his other men wanna break them out."

"Want me to hang around here a while?" Kingdom asked.

"No," Shaye said, "I don't want Doucette to know that you're backing me, yet. Let's keep him guessin'."

"That'll keep his confidence up," Kingdom said, "unless you can jail more of his men."

"Don't worry," Shaye said. "They'll get themselves into trouble. The problem with Doucette's plan, whatever it is, is that he's givin' them time to shoot themselves in the foot."

"Well, okay," Kingdom said, "but I'll be ready to jump in when the time is right — or when things get too hot."

"Appreciate that, Kingdom."

The gunman touched his hat and left the office.

Cole Doucette had found himself a smaller saloon than the Renegade to hang his hat. He was sitting at a table in the Yellow Rose when Sam Hawko and Paul Tayback came in.

"Boss, Sheriff Shaye just locked up two of our boys," Hawko said.

"That so?"

257

"Whataya wanna do about it, boss?" Paul Tayback asked.

"Relax, boys," Doucette said, "I've got this covered. Have a beer."

They went to the bar, got a beer each, then came back and sat down.

"We just gonna leave 'em there?" Hawko asked.

"Who are they?"

"Chet and Roscoe."

"They're stupid," Doucette said, "if I get them out, they'll just get themselves tossed back in again."

"But boss, whatabout —" Tayback started, but Doucette cut him off.

"I'll go and have a talk with the sheriff," he said. "Don't you boys worry about it."

"There's somethin' else," Hawko said.

"What?"

"We just saw Tate Kingdom comin' outta the sheriff's office."

"Again?"

When Doucette had sent Hawko to find out who the man with Shaye was, it had been Kingdom. Now the gunman was in there again.

"What do we do about him?" Tayback asked. "If he decides to take sides —"

"You boys are tryin' to do too much thinkin'," Doucette said. "That's my job.

Just take it easy, stay out of trouble, and wait for my signal."

The two men nodded.

"And go," Doucette added. "Sit somewhere else. I wanna be by myself."

"Sure, boss," Hawko said.

The two men stood up, and then Tayback turned back. "Uh, boss, what's the signal?"

"You'll know when you see it, Tayback," Doucette said. "Now beat it."

FORTY-SIX

Dan Shaye looked up from his desk as his office door opened. He was not surprised to see Cole Doucette enter.

"What brings you around here, Mr. Doucette?" he asked.

"I understand you have a couple of my boys in here, Sheriff."

"That's right."

"You mind tellin' me what you're chargin' them with?"

"Disturbin' the peace."

Doucette nodded. "That sounds about right." He turned to leave.

"You don't want to try to bail them out?" Shaye asked.

"No, no," Doucette said. "Maybe some time in your pokey will teach them a little respect for the law." He smiled. "I know that's what it did for me."

Doucette walked out.

Shaye shook his head. The man was good.

Saying all the right things, but Shaye knew a bad penny when he saw it, and Cole Doucette was as bad as they came. Whatever his plan was, he obviously didn't need the two men in his cells to pull it off.

But Shaye had empty cells, and there were still plenty of Doucette men out there, looking for trouble.

Instead of going back to the Yellow Rose after leaving the sheriff's office, Cole Doucette walked over to the Renegade Saloon. Inside he saw three of his men, two playing poker, one standing at the bar.

He walked up to the one at the bar, took up position next to him and ordered a beer.

"Oh, hey, boss."

"You hear about Chet and Roscoe gettin' locked up, Vin?" Doucette asked.

"Sure did," Vin said. "We gettin' 'em out?"

"No, we're not gettin' 'em out," Doucette said. "They're too stupid to be out."

"Aw, boss —"

"And I don't need the rest of you gettin' stupid, either," Doucette said, cutting him off. "So I want you to go over there and get Ledbetter and Santini out of that game and out of this saloon. Go find someplace to drink that ain't so busy. You got it?"

"I got it, boss."

261

"You know where Hawko and Tayback are?"

"No, sir, I sure don't."

"What about Nils?"

"Ain't seem him."

"Well, find Nils and tell him what I told you."

"Sure, boss," Vin said. "And the others —"

"I got Hawko and Tayback," Doucette said. "Just do what I told you to do."

"Sure, boss. And, uh, when are we makin' a move?"

"You'll all know when to move," Doucette said. "Just wait for my signal."

"And what signal is that, boss?" Vin asked.

"Just go!"

"I'm goin', boss."

Vin walked over to the poker game, leaned in and spoke into each man's ear. They didn't look happy, but they waved at the dealer that they were out, and the three of them left the Renegade.

Doucette drank half his beer and was about to leave when he saw Tate Kingdom at another poker table.

"Hey," he called to the bartender.

"Yeah?"

"Have a girl take Tate Kingdom a beer; tell 'im it's from me." He tossed the money on the bar.

"Yessir."

Doucette picked up his beer and walked to an empty table. As he watched, the bartender gave one of the girls a beer and sent her over to the poker table. She put the beer next to Kingdom, who looked up at her. At that point, she pointed over to where Doucette was sitting.

After she walked away, Kingdom waved at the dealer, took his beer and got up, leaving his chips behind. Obviously, he'd be going back to the table. Then he walked over to Doucette's table.

"Have a seat," Doucette said. "Let's talk."

FORTY-SEVEN

Dan Shaye stood outside the Renegade, saw three of Doucette's men come out. He decided to follow them rather than go inside and see what was happening.

The three men walked on one side of the street, Shaye on the other. He followed along until they reached a smaller, quieter saloon called The Gold Spike. They went inside, and he took up a position across the street. He gave them time to order drinks before he crossed over and stopped just outside the batwing doors, where he could see and hear.

". . . we hadda leave the Renegade," one of them was complaining. "I was about to start winnin'."

"The boss just said we hadda get out," one of the other men said.

The three of them were standing at the bar, holding beers. There were several other men in the place, one at the bar, two seated at tables. The only other occupants were the bartender and one saloon girl. She was young, but tired looking.

"And," the second man said, "he told us to stay outta trouble, or else we'll get tossed in jail like Chet and Roscoe did."

"Ain't we even gonna try to get 'em out?" the third man asked.

"Naw, he said if they was dumb enough to get locked up, they could stay there."

"That ain't right," the third man said, shaking his head. "Just ain't right."

"I should be winnin' money in that poker game," the first man complained again.

Shaye turned away from the door, leaned against the wall next to it. He couldn't see what was going on, but he could still hear them. The way they were grousing, it was only a matter of time before there was some trouble. All he had to do was wait.

Doucette watched as Tate Kingdom walked to his poker game, still carrying his beer mug, and sat down. Then he finished his own beer, stood up and walked out.

He looked up and down the street, didn't see any of his men. Two ladies walked past and he tipped his hat to them and said, "Good day, ladies."

They nodded to him pleasantly and kept

265

walking.

He decided to take a stroll past city hall. Maybe the mayor had a window on the main street, and would see him standing out there. Yeah, that would do for now.

That would do just fine.

Doucette's three men kept drinking a second beer and then, quickly, a third. Before long the saloon began to fill up, and the three men were pushing and shoving each other, still complaining about being sent from the Renegade.

"What about a whorehouse?" one of them said. It sounded like the first man, who'd been playing poker at the Renegade. "There's gotta be a whorehouse in town."

"Ask the bartender," the third man said. "He should know."

"Hey, now," the first man said. "Didn't Doucette tell us to stay away from any cathouses? Yeah, he said that when we first got here."

"So what?" the first man said. "There ain't no poker goin' on in here, and there's only the one saloon girl. I can't stay in this place all night."

"Well," the man who was the voice of reason said, "I ain't goin' to no whorehouse. I ain't gettin' Cole Doucette mad at me."

"I ain't afraid of no Cole Doucette," the first man said.

"Well, you should be."

"Hey," the third man said, "what about this girl? She's kinda weary lookin', but she's young."

"Yeah, she is," the first man said, "and she's got pretty enough hair. Hey, sweetheart, come on over here."

Here it comes, Shaye thought. The waiting was going to be worth it, because these men were all the same. Given enough time, they just made the wrong decision, every time.

Mayor Abner Snow was in his office in the city hall building, sitting at his desk. He still didn't like the idea of hiding in his office or his house, but what else could he do? Shaye was right. He was no match for Cole Doucette.

He took care of some business as the day wore on, but every time there was a knock at the door, he jumped out of his skin, thinking it was Doucette coming to get him.

He stood up, walked to the window and looked down at Main Street. About to turn away, he suddenly saw the man across the street, and froze.

Cole Doucette, looking right up at the window. He saw Snow standing there, and waved. Did the man really expect him to wave back?

He backed away from the window so hard and fast, he banged his hip against his desk. What should he do? Stay there or leave by the back way and go to his house? Did Doucette know where he lived? He probably did. All he had to do was ask somebody.

Everybody in Vengeance Creek knew where the mayor lived!

FORTY-EIGHT

Shaye heard the saloon girl say, "Ow! That hurts. Get off me!"

That was his cue.

He entered the saloon, saw the three men at the bar, one of them holding the girl by the arm. He noticed one of them was not wearing a gun.

"Come on, Ledbetter," one of them said, "let 'er go!"

"Shut up, Vin!" Ledbetter said. "You ain't my boss." It was the young man called Vin who was unarmed.

The third man also reached for the girl.

"Okay, I ain't havin' none of this," Vin said, and backed away.

That suited Shaye. He only had to deal with two.

"I guess your name's Ledbetter," Shaye said, aloud.

Everything in the saloon stopped.

"What of it?" Ledbetter asked.

"And you?" Shaye asked the other man. "What's your name, friend?"

The man hesitated, then said, "Santini." He was dark-skinned, looked Mexican.

"Well, all right, then," Shaye said, "why don't we let the girl go. She's got a job to do."

"I know," Ledbetter, a big, red-faced man, said, "and I want her to do it to me."

"I'm not gonna tell you two men, again," Shaye said. "Let the girl go and come along."

Ledbetter squinted at Shaye, seemed to see the badge for the first time. He might have let up, but the man called Vin spoke up at that moment.

"Better do as he says, Ledbetter."

Apparently, that didn't sit right with the man, being told what to do by Vin.

"We ain't doin' no harm, Sheriff," he said to Shaye. "Why don't you go and bother somebody else?"

Shaye looked at Vin. The man backed up and raised his hands.

"Bartender," Shaye said, "you might wanna move out from behind there."

"Yessir, Sheriff." The man quickly got out from behind the bar.

"Now let's go through this again," Shaye said. "Release the girl, drop your guns and come along."

"Drop my gun?" Ledbetter asked. "Now, that's a new one. You didn't say that before. Do you know who we are, Sheriff?"

"Two big mouths who don't know how to treat a lady," Shaye said.

"This is a lady?" Ledbetter asked.

"In this town, she's a lady," Shaye said, "and she deserves respect."

Ledbetter made a rude noise with his mouth. Shaye noticed that he wore his gun on his right hip, and was holding the girl with his right hand.

"Ledbetter, you're already at a bit of a disadvantage here," Shaye said.

"Howzat?" the man asked, looking confused.

"You're holdin' onto her with your gun-hand," Shaye said. "If you yokels are gonna turn this into a gun battle, you're already dead."

Suddenly, Ledbetter seemed to realize his position. Also, Santini didn't look happy about it. He pulled his hand back from the girl.

"I think we may have pushed this far enough," he said to Ledbetter. "Sheriff, I'm givin' up my gun."

"Put it on the bar," Shaye told Santini, "and push it away."

Santini took the gun out carefully, set it on the bar and then sent it sliding down to the other end.

"Okay, Ledbetter," Shaye said, "the next move is yours."

Abruptly, the bigger man released the girl and put his hands up. The girl darted away from him.

"Like I said, Sheriff," he said, "we wuz only havin' some fun."

"Well, the fun's over," Shaye said. "Take out your gun, put it on the bar and slide it."

Shaye was hoping this would get done without Vin saying another word.

Regretfully, that was not the case.

"Better do as he says, Ledbetter," Vin said, "or he'll kill ya."

"Shut up, Vin!" Ledbetter snapped.

Now that his gunhand was free, Ledbetter might have been having some second thoughts about surrendering his weapon and giving up.

"This ain't right, Sheriff," he complained. "We wuzn't doin' nothin'."

"You were disturbin' the peace," Shaye said, "and maybe there's even an assault charge here."

"Assault?" Ledbetter exploded. "That's crazy!"

"Don't talk yourself out of this, Ledbet-

272

ter," Shaye said. "Give it up."

Shaye watched the man's eyes, and they gave him away. Dan Shaye did not consider himself a fast gun, but he knew when to draw his weapon, and he hit whatever he shot at.

"Yer a sonofabitch," Ledbetter swore, and went for his gun.

FORTY-NINE

Shaye turned the key in the cell door lock, then walked away. He had given Santini his own cell, right next to the other men.

In the office he dropped the keys on his desk and turned to face Vin.

"You better tell your boss he's down to half his men."

"I'll tell 'im, Sheriff," Vin said. "What about Ledbetter's body?"

"I had it taken to the undertaker's," Shaye said. "Doucette can claim it there, if he wants."

"So, I can go?"

"Sure," Shaye said, "you were smart enough to stay out of it. Think you can stay that smart?"

"I'm gonna give it a try," Vin said.

"Then go," Shaye said, "talk to your boss."

"Yessir."

Vin turned and left the office. Shaye took a deep breath, poured himself a cup of coffee, and sat down behind his desk. Things were going okay so far, and he really hadn't had to use his secret weapon yet.

Then he realized he hadn't wondered about his sons in hours.

Feeling he'd put enough of a scare into Mayor Snow, Cole Doucette went back to the Yellow Rose Saloon and sat with a beer. It wasn't long before Vin Packer came in, looking nervous.

"Get a drink first," Doucette said, as the man approached the table. "You look like you're gonna pass out."

Vin went to the bar, got a whiskey, tossed it off, and came back.

"What is it?"

"Santini's in jail."

"I thought he was smarter than that," Doucette said. "What about Ledbetter?"

"Dead," Vin said. "He drew on Sheriff Shaye."

Doucette sat back. "Now I don't know he was that stupid."

"What do we do, boss?"

"You do just what I been tellin' you to do, Vin," Doucette said. "Don't think. Just get yourself a bottle and sit."

Vin went to the bar, bought a bottle, and brought it back to Doucette's table.

"Not here, you idiot," Doucette said. "Somewhere else."

"Awright, right, boss."

He started away, but Doucette said, "Have you seen Hawko and Tayback?"

"No," Vin said, "and not Nils, either."

"Don't worry about him," Doucette said, "I knew he'd get himself in trouble sooner or later." He waved Vin away.

There was a time when Cole Doucette had men he could count on, but that was a long time ago. Now he could only count on himself. But things were progressing as planned. The law had three of his men in jail and one at the undertaker. That ought to make the man pretty confident.

Now Doucette just needed him to become overconfident.

Shaye found the mayor cowering in his house.

"He was at my office!" Snow said.

"Who?"

"Doucette, that's who," the man said.

"He came into your office?"

"No, he was across the street, watching me," Snow said. "Through my window."

"What were you doin' at your window?" Shaye asked. "Givin' him a target?"

"I was just looking down at the street,"

276

Snow said, "and there he was."

"So what did you do?"

"I went out the back and came here," Snow said. "Been here ever since."

"Well, I've got three of his men in jail, and one dead," Shaye said.

"Dead? You killed him?"

"Had to," Shaye said. "He didn't give me a choice."

"How many has he got left?"

"He's got four men besides himself," Shaye said.

"You've cut his force in half!"

"Yes, I have."

Snow frowned.

"You don't sound happy about it."

"It's been too easy."

"But . . . you had to kill one."

"Because he was stupid," Shaye said.

"What are you getting at?"

"I think Doucette knows his men are stupid," Shaye said. "He's got a plan."

"What plan?"

"That's what I'm tryin' to figure out," Shaye said. "I'm puttin' his men away, and he's not blinkin' an eye."

"Which means what?" the mayor asked.

"Which probably means," Shaye said, "that part of his plan is for me to toss all of his men in jail."

"But . . . for what purpose?"

Shaye rubbed his jaw. "To make me over-confident."

"And are you?"

"No," Shaye said.

"But you're confident enough . . . right?"

Shaye didn't answer. Instead he said, "Just stay away from the windows, Mayor," and left.

FIFTY

When morning came, Thomas and James were surprised with a full Mexican breakfast, prepared by the sisters, Elena and Isabella.

They each slept in one of the rooms, after turning down the sisters' offer to share their beds. They were more in need of sleep than sex, even with two such desirable young women.

"That smells good," Thomas said, coming out of the hall into the cantina.

"Please," Elena said, "sit down. It is almost ready."

James came into the room and scolded his brother.

"Why are you makin' these girls cook, after everythin' they been through?"

"No, no, *señor,*" Elena said, "it was our idea. We have done this to thank you."

"Thank us? We probably got your bartender killed, and you could've been next,"

James said.

"You saved us from those *bandidos*," Elena said, "and you saved us from Maximilian."

"Saved you?" Thomas asked, as James sat across from him. "From your bartender?"

"He was a very bad man," Elena said, "and did not treat us well."

"You mean . . ." James said.

"Señor?"

"My brother wants to know if Max . . . took liberties with you and your sister."

"Señor?" She was still puzzled.

"Did Max make you share his bed?" Thomas asked.

"Oh, no, *señor*," Elena said, "he was a terrible man, but he would not have done that."

"Why not?" James asked.

"Maximilian was our papa."

"You mean . . . he made you treat him like a father?" James asked.

"No, *señor*," she said, "he *was* our father. I will go and get the *cafe*."

Elena ran into the kitchen.

"Their father?" James asked. "Even if he was a mean man, they're not all that upset about their father gettin' killed."

"Don't get involved, little brother," Thomas said. "We have our own father to

280

keep happy by bringin' the Fleming boys in."

"Yeah," James said, "we're doin' a great job of that, ain't we?"

"We're still on their trail," Thomas said, "and we've taken care of their men." Thomas rolled some eggs into a tortilla and took a bite. "We're makin' progress."

James grabbed some food and did the same. The girls came out with coffee, and even more food.

"Whoa, whoa," Thomas said, "we've got enough here."

"Please, *señores,*" Isabella said, "eat as much as you like. I will make more."

"Isabella is a wonderful cook," Elena said.

"Yes, she is," Thomas agreed.

"She will make someone a wonderful *esposa.*"

"*Esposa?*" James asked.

"*Si, señor,*" Elena said. "Wife."

Isabella smiled, and then both sisters went back to the kitchen, leaving the brothers staring at each other.

"We better eat quick and get out of here," Thomas sad.

"You said it!"

They finished the food in record time and, with bulging bellies, went out to saddle their

281

horses. The two girls came out and watched them.

"Are you sure you can get those bodies buried?" Thomas asked. "We can do it before we leave."

"You and your brother have done enough, *señor,*" Elena said. "We know some men who will bury them for us."

"You can keep their horses and saddles," James sad, "and any other possessions."

"And their money, *señor?*" Elena asked.

"Yes," Thomas said, "and their money."

The two girls waved happily as the brothers rode away from San Lupita.

They picked up a trail just south of town, but neither brother was expert enough at tracking to know if it was left by the Fleming brothers. It was, however, fairly fresh and heading south.

"We don't have much of a choice," Thomas said. "We can't just ride aimlessly, so we might as well follow these tracks and see where they lead."

"Agreed," James said. "How's your side?"

The girls had cleaned and rebandaged Thomas's wound the night before.

"It hurts, but it's not bleedin', right now," Thomas said.

"You probably shouldn't even be on a horse yet, Thomas," James said.

"Well," Thomas said, "I can't exactly let you chase these two varmints down by yourself, James. Pa would never forgive me."

"And he'd never forgive me if I didn't bring you back alive," James pointed out.

"Well, let's just make him happy and bring the Flemings back."

"Alive?"

Thomas looked off into the distance. "That's gonna be up to them."

FIFTY-ONE

Miles ahead, the Flemings rode side-by-side, having taken the two best horses their gang had.

"You think those four were able to kill 'em?" Harry asked.

"I doubt it," Red said, "but they coulda got lucky."

"We shoulda stayed and helped."

"Not yet, Harry," Red said. "We gotta pick the right place and time, and that little cantina in a little nothin' town wasn't it."

"You ain't afraid, are you, Red?" Harry asked.

"Afraid of what?"

"Them Shaye boys," Harry said.

As an answer Red lashed out and punched Harry in the side of the head. The blow knocked him off his horse, and he hit the ground with a solid thud.

"What the hell?" Harry yelled.

Harry's horse kept moving, so it wasn't

between him and his brother, and Red was able to look down at him.

"You oughtta know better than to ask me a question like that, Harry."

"Ya didn't have to hit me!"

"Yeah, I did," Red said, and began to ride on, leaving Harry to get back to his feet, track down his horse, mount up and follow.

Several hours later, Red and Harry Fleming spotted a dust cloud ahead of them.

"What the hell," Harry said. "They couldn'ta got ahead of us."

"There's only two of them," Red said. "They wouldn't raise that much dust."

"Then who is it?"

"Maybe *federales,*" Red said, "maybe *bandidos.*"

"Jesus," Harry said, "which ones would be worse?"

"I guess we're gonna find out," Red said. "Make sure you let me do the talkin' Harry, understand?"

"I understand, Red," Harry said. "Just don't hit me again. My face and butt are still sore from the last time."

"Two things, Harry," Red said. "Don't say anythin', and if you do, don't say anythin' stupid."

"I'll let you do the talkin', Red," Harry

said. "Don't worry about that."

But Red *was* worried about that. Harry had a short temper, and it always got him in trouble, as evidenced by what had happened in Vengeance Creek.

"If it's *federales,*" Red said, "we could end up in jail."

"And if it's *bandidos*?" Harry asked.

"We could end up dead."

"Then don't worry, Red," Harry assured his brother, "I ain't gonna say a word."

The brothers rode at a leisurely pace, and when the riders came over a hill they saw that it was a company of *federales.*

"Red —" Harry said.

"Stay calm," Red said. "I've been down here before, remember? Just keep quiet."

Red reined his horse in and his brother followed his example. They sat there and waited for the Mexican police to reach them.

The man at the head of the column of eight soldiers held his hand up and reined in his horse in front of Red and Harry Fleming. Red could tell from his insignia that he was a captain. He appeared to be in his early thirties, certainly too young for a higher rank, but Red said, "Good day, Colonel."

"It is Capitan," the man said, "Capitan

Enrique Domingo Salazar, of his Excellency Presidente Porfirio Diaz's Federales."

"My mistake, Capitan."

"What are your names?"

"I'm Red Fleming, and this is my brother, Harry."

"What are you *gringos* doing in Mexico?"

"We're on the run, Capitan."

"Red —" Harry said, but Red continued and cut his brother off.

"We've got a couple of American lawmen on our trail."

The captain frowned. "Did they follow you into Mexico?"

"They sure did," Red said. "In fact, they've already killed four of our friends."

"Well," Capitan Salazar said, "you and your brother are not wanted in Mexico, are you?"

"I assure you we're not, Capitan," Red said. "We're just here lookin' for a little sanctuary."

"As long as you do not break our Mexican laws, you are welcome," Salazar said, "but these American lawmen who followed you . . . who are they?"

"They're deputy sheriffs from Vengeance Creek," Red said, "the Shaye brothers from Vengeance Creek."

"They are not deputies here in Mexico,"

Salazar said. "And we do not appreciate *gringo* lawmen bringing their badges into our country."

"Well," Red said, "they're just a few hours behind us. I'm sure you won't have any trouble findin' them."

"And find them we shall," Capitan Salazar assured him. "Remember, break no laws in Mexico, *señor.*"

"We won't, Capitan," Red Fleming said. "That's a promise."

Salazar looked behind him, waved to his men, then rode around the two outlaw brothers, followed by the column, each member of which ignored them.

"Jesus Christ," Harry said, "why'd you tell him we were on the run?"

"You heard him," Red said. "As long as we don't break the law in Mexico, we don't have a problem. They hate it when lawmen from the United States come into their country without permission."

"Permission?"

"Sure," Red said, "some lawmen petition the *federales* for permission to come in and hunt."

"But the Shayes didn't do that."

"I doubt they had time to," Red said.

"So they're gonna be in trouble when those *federales* find them."

"They sure are," Red said. "And we'll be free and in the clear."

"So where are we goin' now?" Harry asked.

"Oh, I don't know," Red said, "maybe we'll just keep ridin' until we get to Mexico City."

"You been there before?" Harry asked.

"Nope," Red said, "but I've heard a lot about it. I always wanted to have a look-see."

"How far is it?"

"Pretty far," Red said, "but we can take our time." He looked behind them as the column of soldiers disappeared over a rise. "I think they're gonna take care of our problem with the Shaye deputies."

FIFTY-TWO

"Where do you think these tracks are headed?" James asked.

"I don't know, James," Thomas said. "I ain't never been down here. Pa's been to Mexico, but he ain't here. Now."

"I wonder where we'd get to if we just keep goin' in this direction."

"Maybe Mexico City," Thomas said.

"You think the Flemings might go that far?"

"Why not?" Thomas said. "They're lookin' for a place to hide out, ain't they?"

"What the heck is that?" James said, pointing.

"It's a cloud of dust," Thomas said. "Somebody's comin' this way."

"You think they turned around?" James asked.

"No," Thomas said, "that's too much dust for two men."

"Then . . . who?" James asked. "I hope it

ain't *bandidos*."

They had their badges in their pockets, so if it was bandits coming, they wouldn't know they were lawmen. But that didn't mean they wouldn't try to rob and maybe kill them.

"We better get out of sight," Thomas said.

"But where?"

They looked around. The ground around them was rolling with peaks and valleys, but they needed something high or deep enough to hide behind.

"Let's try over there," Thomas suggested, pointing. "Looks like there's a drop off."

They rode to where Thomas had been pointing and found what they needed.

"Looks like a dry creek bed," James said.

"Deeper," Thomas said, "maybe from a dried up stream or even river. But it's what we need. Get off your horse."

They dismounted and led their horses by the reins down into the dry bed.

"Keep 'em quiet," Thomas told James.

"What are you gonna do?"

"I wanna see who we're hidin' from."

Thomas climbed back up, but only far enough so he could peer over the edge. At that moment the riders came into view, and they were not bandits.

They were *federales*!

"Who is it?" James hissed.

"Shhh." Thomas slid back down. "It's a company of *federales*," he whispered.

"Then why are we hidin'?" James asked. "They're lawmen, and so are we."

"They're lawmen, all right," Thomas said, "but we ain't, remember?"

"Oh, yeah."

"Let's keep quiet until they pass."

The brothers fell silent, listening to the sound of the horses riding by. Eventually, the hoofbeats faded away, and they relaxed a bit.

"Pa says the Mexicans hate American lawmen," Thomas said, "especially when they cross the border without permission."

"Like we did."

"Right."

"You think they saw the Flemings?"

"I think they did," Thomas said, as something occurred to him. "You know, they ain't wanted down here, and they probably told the *federales* about us."

"So they could use the Mexican police to get rid of us!"

Thomas nodded.

"That's a dirty trick," James said.

"And smart," Thomas said, "real smart."

"Then it wasn't Harry's idea," James said. "We had him in jail long enough to find out

292

how dumb he was."

"That's right," Thomas said, "so Red's the smart one."

"I guess so."

"Sure," Thomas said, "the older brother is always the smart one."

He grabbed his horse's reins and started walking it back up the slope.

"Hey!" James yelled.

FIFTY-THREE

Dan Shaye turned the key in the cell door on the man named Nils, and now he had taken care of five of Doucette's men. Nils had started trouble at the whorehouse, and Miss Lizzie, the Madam, had sent her Negro piano player to fetch Sheriff Shaye.

"He got rough with one of my girls," she told him, when he arrived. That was all he needed to haul the man's ass off to jail.

He came out of the cell block, hung the key on the wall peg, and sat behind his desk. That left Doucette with three men still walking around free: the two Shaye had met before — Hawko and Tayback — and the one called Vin.

Hawko and Tayback were the men Mayor Snow had tried to saddle him with as temporary deputies. Turned out they were working for Doucette all along. It was a good thing Shaye had turned them down and kicked them out of town.

Wait a minute . . .

That was right. He kicked them out of town, and now they were back. He could toss them in jail for that, call it . . . trespassing. Couldn't he?

He figured before he did that, he'd better make sure he could make the charge stick — if it was a legal charge. Judge Fairly could tell him that.

Shaye didn't have much use for Judge Fairly. He was simply a friend and lackey of Mayor Snow's, but he'd have the legal issues at his fingertips.

Judge Fairly was in his office at the courthouse when Shaye arrived. His clerk told him that the sheriff needed to see him, and Fairly consented to an audience — reluctantly.

"I have a lot of work, Shaye," he said, gruffly. "What's so important?"

Fairly was in his late fifties, a man who kept himself neat and fit. His hair and mustache were trimmed almost daily.

"I have some legal issues I need to check with you, Judge," Shaye said. "They're on behalf of the mayor."

At the mention of the mayor, the judge stopped playing with the papers on his desk and looked directly at Shaye.

"Why didn't you say so?" he asked. "Have a seat."

Shaye sat across the desk from the judge. He knew the papers on the man's desk were probably pointless, just props to make the man look busy when he wasn't.

Shaye went on to tell the judge that he had men in his jail cells on trumped-up charges, and asked about the charge he was thinking of using on Hawko and Tayback. He also told him that would then leave Cole Doucette with only one man available to him.

Since Fairly was friends with Snow, he knew what the situation was with Cole Doucette.

"Why don't you just trump up a charge on Doucette and toss him in jail?"

"I wouldn't be able to keep him there long, Judge," Shaye said. "You know that. A good lawyer would get him out."

"I could keep him in," Fairly pointed out.

"That's true, Judge, but knowing you, eventually you'd have to go by the letter of the law. I mean," Shaye said, almost choking, "that's the kind of man you are."

Fairly cleared his throat before speaking. "Yes, well, a halfway decent lawyer will get these other fellas out, as well."

"But maybe not until I've dealt with Dou-cette."

"And how'd you plan on dealin' with the man?" Fairly asked.

"I haven't decided yet," Shaye said, "but I'd like him to not have much in the way of back-up when I do."

"Sounds like a cat'n'mouse game to me."

"You're probably right, Judge."

"Well," the judge said, "lock these other men up for trespassing, and if the case comes up, I'll rule in your favor. We'll keep these men off the streets as long as we can."

"That was my hope, Judge," Shaye said, standing. "Thank you."

"Yes, yes, of course," Fairly said. "The last thing we want is for our illustrious mayor to get shot."

"Exactly what I was thinkin', Judge."

"Well," Judge Fairly said, looking surprised, "it isn't every day you and I are on the same page, is it, Sheriff."

"No, sir, it sure isn't," Shaye agreed, "but I'm glad we see eye to eye on this. So will the mayor. I'll let you get back to work."

"Oh, yes," the judge said, once again grabbing some papers from his desk. Shaye made his way to the door, eager to leave.

In front of the building Shaye stopped and

considered his next move. Actually, a bath wouldn't be a bad idea, since he felt dirty from kowtowing to the judge the way he had. Still, he had gotten what he wanted. Now he needed to locate Hawko and Tayback and, somehow, get the jump on them. Hopefully, bringing them in wouldn't lead to gun play.

FIFTY-FOUR

Shaye walked around town, trying to locate Hawko and Tayback. He tried three saloons and didn't find them. He was starting to think Doucette had instructed them to stay out of sight.

When he checked the Yellow Rose, he peered in over the batwing doors and saw Doucette seated at a table with a beer, and his man Vin standing at the bar. They probably didn't even know yet that he had locked up Nils. He decided to fill Doucette in.

He entered the saloon. It was still early, so there were hardly any drinkers in the place. In fact, since the word had gotten around that Doucette was using the place as a kind of headquarters, business had slowed down even more.

The outlaw looked up from his mug as Shaye entered, and he smiled.

"Well, Sheriff," he called out, "grab a beer

on me. Come and have a seat."

Shaye thought about what the judge had said about cat'n'mouse. That was exactly what was going on.

"Don't mind if I do," Shaye said.

He collected a mug of beer from the bartender and carried it over to Doucette's table.

"Were you lookin' for me?" Doucette asked.

"Actually," Shaye said, "I was lookin' for two of your men, Hawko and Tayback."

"Now don't tell me they got themselves into trouble," Doucette said. "Your jail is gonna be brimmin' with my men, Sheriff."

"It already is," Shaye said. "I just put Nils in there."

"And what did he do?"

"Got rough with one of the girls at the whorehouse."

Doucette shook his head.

"I told my boys to stay away from that place," Doucette said. "Nothin' but evil in whorehouses."

"That may be true."

"So why do you want Hawko and Tayback?"

"They were in town a while back — probably as advance scouts for you — and I ran them out."

"I heard about that."

"Well, they shouldn't be here now," Shaye said. "They shouldn't be back in town without my say-so."

"And so you're gonna lock them up for . . ."

"Trespassing."

"Trespassing!" Doucette repeated. "And I bet you got a judge who'll back that up."

"Yes, I do."

Doucette looked over at Vin. "What're you gonna do about him? He's been nothin' but law abidin' since we got here."

"He has," Shaye agreed. "He might be your smartest man."

"Hear that, Vin?" Doucette called out. "The sheriff here gives you credit for brains. Well, more brains than those other idiots, anyway."

Vin didn't know what to say to that, so he just raised his beer mug.

"And last but not least," Doucette said, "there's me. What're you gonna lock me up for, Sheriff?"

"I don't plan to lock you up, Cole," Shaye said. "I'm just gonna see what your next move is gonna be."

"And what if my next move is just to . . . have another beer?" Doucette asked.

"Oh, I think it'll be somethin' a little more

active than that," Shaye said. "See, despite what you say, I think you're here for Mayor Snow. And I aim to see to it that you don't get him."

"You mean you think I'm lyin' about not holdin' a grudge?" Doucette asked. "Tsk, tsk, tsk," he clucked his tongue. "That's not very Christian of you, Sheriff."

"I'm not a Christian, Cole," Shaye said, "and I'm willin' to bet neither are you."

Doucette laughed. "You got that right, Sheriff. I'm not a Christian, or a religious man of any kind. You know why? There's no religion in prison, only brutality."

Shaye didn't respond to that. He knew a lot of men who had gone to prison and found religion there. But this was not a point to be argued with Cole Doucette.

"My religion, if I had one while I was inside," Doucette went on, "would have been revenge."

"And that's not somethin' you'd forget so easily," Shaye said.

"No, you'd think not," Doucette said. "So are you expectin' that when you have all my men in jail I won't go after the judge," Doucette asked, "or I will?"

"I told you," Shaye said, "I don't know what you're gonna do. I'm waitin' to see."

"Well," Doucette said, "I guess you better

just keep on lookin' for Hawko and Tayback, then. Toss them into one of your cells, and we'll see what happens after that, hum?"

Shaye stood up, left his full mug of beer, untouched, on the table.

"Yeah, I guess we'll see."

As Shaye went back through the batwing doors, Doucette reached across the table and grabbed his beer.

"No point in lettin' this go to waste."

FIFTY-FIVE

Within the hour, Shaye found Hawko and Tayback . . .

They weren't staying in any of the town's hotels, and they weren't drinking in the saloons. They were seated on the porch of a boarding house they'd found rooms in, passing a bottle of whiskey back and forth and grousing.

"I don't like bein' told to stay away from saloons and whorehouses," Tayback said. "What other reason is there to go to any town?"

"Doucette's payin' the bills," Hawko pointed out. "Until he isn't, we have to do what he wants."

"Yeah, well . . . where's he gettin' all this money to pay us with? And the others? I mean, didn't he just get out of prison?"

"Who knows?" Hawko said. "Maybe he had the money hidden away before he went inside."

They passed the bottle several more times, and then got to the bottom of it.

"We need another bottle," Tayback said.

"Well, we can't go to a saloon."

"There's a mercantile a few blocks from here. I saw it earlier today. I bet they got whiskey."

"Okay," Hawko said, "we go and get a bottle and come right back here."

"What about the old lady who runs this place?" Tayback asked, as they stood up. "Maybe she's still got a few miles left in her."

"Oh Jesus," Hawko said, "she's gotta be fifty if she's a day."

They staggered off the porch and started walking back toward town.

. . . and that's where Shaye finally ran into them, coming out of the mercantile, each cradling a bottle.

"Hello, boys," he said.

They stopped short and stared at him.

"Whataya want, Sheriff?" Tayback asked. "We're busy."

"Yeah," Hawko said, "we ain't hurtin' nobody. We're jus' takin' these bottles back to our rooming house."

"I seem to remember runnin' you two out of town a while back."

"You did," Hawko said, "and that wasn't very nice of you. We wuz jus' tryin' to get jobs as temporary deputies that time."

"Yeah," Tayback said, "we wuz tryin' to help you and your mayor."

"But you were really workin' for Cole Doucette."

"So?" Hawko said. "A man can work for two people."

"You couldn't very well be deputies if the men I needed as deputies were goin' to go against Doucette."

Tayback started to laugh and Hawko joined in.

"He's got a point," Tayback said.

"So I need you boys to give up your guns and come with me to jail. You can even bring your bottles."

"We can?" Hawko asked.

"Sure," Shaye said. "After all, you can drink anywhere. And you can share with your friends who are already there."

"Say, that's right," Tayback said, looking at Hawko. "He's got our buddies in his jail."

"That ain't real nice of you, Sheriff," Hawko said. "You're leavin' our employer without no back-up."

"He's got Vin."

The two men laughed again.

"Vin?" Tayback asked. "He don't know

one end of a gun from the other."

"You don't know who he's got," Hawko said, still laughing. "You're in for a surprise."

"Shhhh," Tayback said to his friend, putting his finger over his lips. "Ya gotta keep quiet."

"Quiet about what?" Shaye asked.

"Naw, naw, naw," Hawko said. "We ain't gonna say no more about it, Sheriff."

"Yeah," Tayback whispered, "it's a secret."

Okay, then, they left him only one choice.

"Whataya say, boys? Guns?"

The two drunk men looked at each other, and then shook their heads.

"No guns, Sheriff," Hawko said. "Sorry."

"I'm sorry, too," Shaye said. "You're both under arrest."

"For what?" Hawko demanded.

"Trespassing," Shaye said. "You never should've come back to town."

"What the hell —" Tayback said.

"We ain't goin' with you, Sheriff," Hawko said.

"Yeah," Shaye said, putting his hand on his gun, "you are."

The two friends looked at each other, smiled, then dropped their bottles and went for their guns.

They were drunk, but Shaye couldn't afford to take that into account. What he knew for a fact was that two men were drawing down on him, and he had no idea how accurate their shots would be in their condition.

But he knew how accurate he was.

Always.

FIFTY-SIX

Shaye left the undertaker's office after seeing to the delivery of the bodies of Hawko and Tayback. He now had four of Doucette's men locked up, and had killed three of them. There was only Doucette and Vin left, but Hawko and Tayback had indicated there was a surprise in store for Shaye. Did that mean another man? More men on the way? Was that what Doucette was waiting for?

Shaye heard the sound of boots on the boardwalk. Quite a few townspeople had walked by him, nodding or exchanging a greeting, but these footsteps sounded different. He turned and saw Tate Kingdom coming toward him.

"I heard about the shootin'," the gunman said. "You okay?"

"I'm fine," Shaye said. "It's two of Doucette's men who are inside."

"Well," Kingdom said, "you keep up this

pace, and you won't need my help at all."

"That would be fine with me," Shaye said. "I'd be very happy handlin' all of this on my own."

"And do you think that's going to happen?"

"I doubt it," Shaye said. "Doucette doesn't seem to be alarmed about any of this."

"And that bothers you?"

"To no end."

"It would seem if he's that calm, he must be planning something."

"And all I can do is wait him out."

"Can you keep his men in jail that long?" Kingdom asked.

"With the help of the local judge, yes, but not forever."

"Well . . ."

"Well what?"

"You could stage a jail break," Kingdom suggested, "and just kill them in the process."

"I'm afraid that's not an option," Shaye said.

"It was just a suggestion." Kingdom gave the front of the undertaker's a good, long look, then said, "I'll be in the Renegade if you want me."

"Thanks."

Shaye watched the gunman walk away,

disturbed by the fact that he had already thought of the jail break idea himself.

Shaye sat in his office later. There was no point in double shifts on his rounds anymore. For one thing, he still thought about Thomas and James, wondering where they were and what they were doing. Had he made the right decision, sending them out separately the way he had? And second, there were no more of Doucette's men to keep an eye on.

And the ones in his cells were making their presence known, complaining loudly about being hungry, and having been locked up for no reason. He also heard them talking amongst themselves, complaining that Doucette wasn't doing anything to get them out. They were so displeased with their boss that Shaye was tempted to release them, figuring they might leave town. But he decided against it. Might as well wait until the whole ugly business was over.

"Boss?"

Cole Doucette looked up from his mug of beer and saw Vin standing there.

"What?"

"Um, I know you got a plan, boss," Vin

311

said, "but we got three men dead and four in jail."

"Vin, do you think you're tellin' me somethin' I don't already know?"

"Well, no, but —"

"There ain't no 'buts,'" Doucette told him. "You're the last man standin', Vin. Now it's gonna be up to you and me."

"That's okay with me, boss, but . . . what's gonna be up to you and me? What are we gonna do?"

"We're gonna do what we came here to do," Doucette said, "what I told you all in the beginnin' was my goal. Do you remember that?"

"Sure I do, but —"

"What did I say?"

"You wuz out for revenge."

"And I'm gonna get it," Doucette said. "You can believe in that, Vin."

"I do, boss, but —"

"Then stop sayin' but and do what I've been tellin' you to do."

"Just wait for your signal?"

"That's right."

"Can I go get somethin' to eat?"

"You know what, Vin?" Doucette stood up. "Why don't we both go and get somethin' to eat."

"Where, boss?"

Doucette put his hand on the younger man's shoulder and said, "I know just the place."

When Cole Doucette and Vin walked into the Rawhide Steak House, they had been in town long enough for everybody to know who they were. That was why it got very, very quiet as they stood inside the door, waiting to be seated.

"Uh, just the two of you gentlemen?" one of the waiters asked.

"That's right," Doucette said.

"This way, please."

The waiter showed them to a table and handed them menus, then scurried away. The other diners in the place were watching the men with interest.

Doucette looked around and stared back at them. He didn't see Mayor Snow there anywhere. That was too bad. He really wanted to make the man sweat before he finally killed him.

"This is a nice place," Vin commented.

"Too fancy for you, Vin?" Doucette asked.

"No, no, this is fine," Vin said. "It's just that . . ." he leaned forward and lowered his voice, ". . . everybody's lookin' at us."

"They're not lookin' at us, Vin," Doucette whispered back, "they're lookin' at me."

"Oh," Vin said.

"So don't let that ruin your meal," Doucette said. "Order anythin' you want. It's on me."

"Thanks, boss."

"Yeah," Doucette said, "have the biggest steak they've got. It ain't like we're gonna pay for it."

"We're not?"

Doucette shook his head. He had no intention of paying for this meal, and that was only the beginning.

FIFTY-SEVEN

Doucette and Vin each had a huge steak dinner, followed by pie and coffee for dessert.

"So what are we gonna do, just walk out?" Vin asked, as they finished their pie.

"We came to this town to kill a man, Vin," Doucette said. "Tell me not payin' for a meal bothers you more than that."

"Hey, I jus' mean that feller, he deserves to die for what he done to you," Vin said. "This was a real good meal. They deserve to get paid for it."

Doucette stared across the table at the younger man, the only one of his men left who was out of jail or alive.

"You know what, Vin?" he asked. "You're right."

"Huh? I am?"

"Sure," Doucette said, "and just to make you feel better, we'll pay for the meal. Howzat strike you?"

"That's, uh, real good, boss." Vin wasn't all that sure, though. He wondered if Doucette was going to leave it to him to pay the bill. That wouldn't be good, because he had no money.

Doucette waved the waiter over.

"Sir?"

"The check, please."

"Of course, sir."

When the check came, Doucette made a show of taking out his money and setting it on the table.

"See?" he said to Vin.

"I see," Vin said. "Thanks, boss."

Outside, in front of the restaurant, Doucette said to Vin, "I think it may be time to make our move."

"Should I get my gun?"

"Yeah," Doucette said, "strap it on. And wait for my signal."

"Yessir."

Doucette looked at Vin.

"Are you ready?"

"Ready as I'll ever be."

"This could be reputation-making, you know."

"I know," Vin said.

"Go on," Doucette said. "I'll see you later."

"Thanks for the steak, boss."

"Sure. Hey!"

Vin turned.

"Make sure you stay out of trouble."

"Yessir."

Doucette watched as Vin headed for the hotel, where he had a room. The kid was the least experienced of all his men, but the most talented. In the end, this was going to be very, very interesting.

Shaye heard about Doucette and his man Vin eating at the Rawhide Steak House. He figured Doucette was still trying to put a scare into Mayor Snow, thinking the man might be having supper there.

Maybe it was time to put an end to this once and for all. Time to push Doucette into making his move.

FIFTY-EIGHT

Thomas and James rode into the town of Poco Diablo, feeling like they were dragging their asses behind them. The Mexican heat had been baking them for days, and they each needed a drink.

"This is takin' too damn long," James complained, "and we're too deep into Mexico."

They'd been avoiding *federales* troops the whole way, and once had to take cover to avoid running into a pack of bandits.

"Maybe we'll get some word here," Thomas said.

"We don't know that they even came this way," James said. "Why are there so many damn tracks in Mexico?"

"*Federales* patrols, *bandidos,* travelers," Thomas said. "Also the fact that you and me, we're not trackers."

"I know it!" James snapped, then said, "Sorry."

They rode down the quiet street, looking around.

"Why is it every time we ride into some Mexican town, it's *siesta* time?" James asked.

"It's always *siesta* time in Mexico," Thomas said.

"Seems like it."

They rode up to the front of a cantina and dismounted, still cautiously looking around.

"I'm tired of these little cantinas," James said. "I want a steak."

"When we get back to the good ol' U.S. of A. I'll buy you the biggest steak you ever saw."

"I'm gonna hold you to that."

As they approached the door, there came the sound of gunfire and bullets striking the walls and windows around them. They dove for the most cover they could find, the inside of the cantina.

"Jesus!" James said, drawing his gun.

Thomas did the same thing, and they braced their backs against the walls on either side of the door. They looked around the cantina and found that it was completely empty.

"What the hell —" James said.

"Not *siesta* time," Thomas said. "Bushwhackin' time."

"This place is empty."

"And the street is empty," Thomas said. "Seems like the town knew what was comin'."

"Yeah, well, too bad we didn't."

"Are you hit?" Thomas asked.

James patted his torso, then took off his hat and saw the hole in it.

"Damn close," he said, putting it back on, "but no."

"Me, neither," Thomas said.

"Think it's the Flemings?" James asked.

"I hope it is," Thomas said. "If it's just some Comancheros or *bandidos* they hired to kill us, then we're fallin' even farther behind."

"Well there ain't much we can do about that," James said, "we're pinned down. Where's the damn law in this town?"

"Maybe he's in on it."

"That's great!"

Thomas risked a look around the edge of the doorway. Their horses were still standing where they'd left them.

"I wish we had our rifles," he said.

"Maybe there's somethin' behind the bar."

"Take a look."

James crawled over to the bar, got behind it and reached beneath it.

"I got this," he said, coming out with a

shotgun. "Twelve gauge side-by-side."

"Hang onto it."

James crawled back to his wall, holding the shotgun ready, holstering his pistol.

"Now what?" he asked.

"Now we wait," Thomas said. "The Flemings probably set this up. We'll just wait for them to call the tune."

"What about a back door?"

"We can check," Thomas said, "but if there is one, they've probably got it covered."

"I'll check the bar," James said. "You check for a back door."

"Okay."

Thomas crawled away from the front of the cantina, then got to his feet. He found a doorway into a back storage room. No rooms for rent there. He saw a back door and walked to it. He opened the door a crack, waited, then opened it a little wider. Immediately, there were several shots. He slammed the door shut as lead slammed into it.

Back in the cantina, he crawled to his front wall again.

"The back door's covered," he said.

"I heard."

Thomas risked another peek outside. The street was still empty.

"All right," he said, drawing his head back, "let's see what happens over the next few minutes, and then we'll come up with a plan."

"We will?"

"Yes, James," Thomas said, "we will. After all, Pa always has a plan."

"Yeah," James said, "but he's Pa."

FIFTY-NINE

A couple of days earlier, Red and Harry Fleming arrived in Poco Diablo, stopped in to see the sheriff right away.

"Ah, *mis amigos,*" Sheriff Pedro Arroyo greeted them. As always, he had a big smile dotted with gold teeth. "Welcome back to Poco Diablo."

Red walked to the desk, dropped some money down on it.

"Ah, *gracias,*" Arroyo said. He swept the money off the desk top and into a drawer. "What can I do for you, *señor*? It has been some time since you were here last."

"You been here before, Red?" Harry asked.

"A few times, Harry," Red said. "Now just shut up a minute." He looked at Arroyo, who seemed to have aged ten years since he'd last seen him. He knew the man had to be near fifty, but he looked almost seventy.

"I just need you to stay out of the way, Pedro," Red said, "as always."

"*Si, señor,*" Arroyo said, "that is what you always want."

"Well, we're gonna need it now more than ever," Red said. "See, we're gonna kill us a couple of American lawmen, here."

"*Aieee,*" Arroyo said, sitting back in his chair. "That may take a little more of your American money, *Señor* Red."

"Why?" Harry demanded. "They ain't lawmen here."

"But someone will come looking, no?" Arroyo asked.

"Possibly," Red said. "Don't worry, there'll be more money."

"Ah, excellent!"

"Are there more *gringos* in town?" Red asked.

"*Si, señor,*" Arroyo said, "they are in the cantina. They said they were waiting for you."

"They said right," Red said. "Thanks, Pedro."

"*Si, señor.*"

Red turned to Harry. "Come on, the rest of the boys are here."

Harry didn't know his brother was taking him to Poco Diablo to meet more men. That was Red's plan all along, to lure the lawmen further into Mexico, and kill them there.

There were four men waiting for them at the cantina when they got there. They greeted Red boisterously, with lots of slaps on the back. Harry didn't know any of them.

"Is this him?" one of them asked. "This is the little brother?"

"That's him," Red said. "Harry, meet Tom Gareth. We've worked together on and off for more than ten years."

Gareth slapped Harry on the back. "Glad to meet ya, son." Gareth was about Red's age, ten or twelve years older than Harry.

Gareth pointed and said, "That's Cutler, that's Shaw and that's Tutt."

The three men, all in their thirties, waved with one hand, held beers with the other.

"You got my telegram?" Red asked Gareth.

"Got it," Gareth said. "Killin' two lawmen and gettin' away with it will be worth the long ride down here. Besides, I love Mexican women."

"All right, then," Red said. "Let's get a drink and we'll go over the plan. They're probably a day behind us, maybe less . . ."

"So we're just gonna sit here and wait for

'em?" Gareth asked, some time later.

Red looked at the man over his glass of tequila. "No, we're gonna wait across the street. By the time they ride in, they'll be ready for a drink. Their first stop will be this cantina."

"And then it'll be their last stop, right?" Harry asked.

Red looked at his brother. "It will be if we do this right and nobody jumps the gun."

"Whataya lookin' at me for?" Harry complained.

"Because you get excited, Harry," Red said. "You're gonna hafta stay calm, and not fire until I do. Understand?"

"Sure, I understand, Red," Harry said. "I ain't stupid."

"You sure act it sometimes."

"Hey!"

Red reached out and mussed his little brother's hair.

"Take it easy," he said. "I'm just jokin'." But the look he exchanged with Gareth said he wasn't joking. Red knew his brother was stupid and acted rashly, because that's how they got into this mess in the first place.

"So whatta we do in the meantime?" Gareth asked.

"You go ahead and enjoy your Mexican women," Red said. "Let's just put a man on watch so we get a warnin' when they're approaching town. And, oh yeah . . . keep your men sober!"

Gareth looked over at the other table, where his men were passing around a bottle of tequila.

"Don't worry," he assured Red, "that's their last bottle until after it's over."

"It better be," Red said.

A full day later, Harry Fleming got excited when he saw Thomas Shaye's back and fired too soon . . .

SIXTY

Shaye left his office, intending to find Doucette and, hopefully, have it out with him. With most of his men in jail or dead, he had very little backing. Maybe Daniel could convince him to leave town — but he doubted it.

He found the man sitting in front of the hotel, leaning his chair back against the wall, seemingly relaxed.

" 'Afternoon, Sheriff," Doucette greeted.

"Doucette," Shaye said. "You're lookin' pretty content."

"And why not? It's a beautiful day."

"And probably your last in town," Shaye said. "At least, your last without bein' behind bars."

"That's so?" Doucette asked.

"Up to now I've been content to wait for you to make a move, but I gotta give it to you. You outlasted me. I need you to ride out of town or show me a reason why not?"

"The reason why not," Doucette said, "is I haven't done what I came here to do."

"Kill Abner Snow."

"That's it," Doucette said. "I've scared him pretty good, don't you think?"

"You've scared him a lot."

"Yeah," Doucette said, "that part's been fun, but I've got to give you credit, Sheriff. You almost outwaited me. Seems like we both ran out of patience on the same day."

Shaye put one foot up on the boardwalk and leaned his left shoulder against a post, leaving his gun arm free.

"So, whataya say, Doucette? What's it gonna be?"

"Well," Doucette said, looking off into the distance as if seeking some inner guidance, "it doesn't seem right for me to leave before I'm done, so I guess that isn't going to happen."

"Have it your way," Shaye said. "Let me have your gun and we'll go and join your men in the jail."

"And how long do you think you can keep me there?"

"I don't know," Shaye said. "I guess we're gonna find out."

"Well, I don't think so," Doucette said. "Vin?"

From out of the lobby came the young

329

man Shaye only knew as Vin. He looked as young and innocent as he had looked all week, except for one thing — now he was wearing a gun on his hip.

"Shaye, you know my man Vin."

"Mr. Shaye," Vin said.

"So he's got you wearin' a gun now, son?" Shaye asked.

"Oh, I usually wear a gun, Sheriff," Vin said. "Mr. Doucette actually had me take it off just before we got to town."

"I see." Shaye looked at Doucette. "You havin' babies fight your fights for you now, Doucette?"

"Oh, he looks like a baby, Sheriff," Doucette said, "but he ain't. See, I had a cellmate in prison who told me his son was a natural-born gunhand. Ever since he was a small boy, he could handle a gun like nobody you ever saw. When I got out of prison, I went and looked him up. That's why it took me so long to get here. I had to go and take a look at Vin myself, and then convince him to come along. But here he is. This kid is the fastest gun I've ever seen."

"Is that a fact?" Shaye asked.

"Oh yeah, it is," Doucette said. "And he's gonna show you." Doucette smiled. "You don't look worried. Still a little overconfident because you took care of the rest of my men so easily. I knew you would. See, I only brought them along to give you something to do, and to let Vin watch you."

"I seen how you handle yourself, Sheriff," Vin said. "You're a good man. I'm gonna be sorry to kill you."

"Vin," Shaye said, "you're lettin' this man turn you into somethin' you really aren't cut out to be. You ever kill a man before?"

"Oh, I checked on that, too," Doucette said. "He's only in his early twenties, and he's already killed nine men in fair fights. Just plain outslicked 'em. You'll be number ten, the biggest. He'll have a reputation after he kills you."

Shaye looked at Vin, who seemed very relaxed.

"You really want to do this, son?"

"I kinda have to, Sheriff," Vin said. "It's my next step in growin' up."

"Did Doucette convince you of that?"

"Oh, no," Vin said, "I knew I'd have to face somebody with a reputation sometime. I'm just sorry it's you."

"And no time like the present," Doucette said.

"I don't have a reputation as a fast gun, Doucette," Shaye said. "As a matter of fact, my son Thomas is faster than I ever was."

"But he's not here, is he?" Doucette

331

asked. "So you're elected, Sheriff." Doucette turned his head, but kept his eyes on Shaye. "Vin?"

"Don't we need a big crowd, Mr. Doucette?"

"Don't worry, son," Doucette said. "When it's over, there'll be a crowd, and everyone will know who killed Sheriff Dan Shaye in a fair fight."

Vin looked at Shaye, then stepped down into the street.

SIXTY-ONE

"Did you notice somethin'?" Thomas asked.

"Like what?" James asked.

"The first shot," Thomas said. "I moved after the first shot, and then the volley started."

"I wondered how they could've missed with so many bullets flyin'," James said. "I ducked for cover when you did. I just heard a bunch of shots."

"Well, I heard one, and then the rest."

"What's that mean?"

"Somebody got antsy and fired too soon," Thomas said. "That's the only reason we're alive."

James sneaked a look outside, didn't see anyone.

"We'll have to find out who that was and thank him," he said.

"Yeah," Thomas said, "we'll do that as soon as we get out of this mess."

"I could use a drink," James said, staring

at the bar. "It's goddamned hot in here."

"Help yourself."

James once again crawled to the bar, returned with a bottle of tequila. He took a swig, then held it up, asking his brother if he wanted any.

"If you can hand it to me without gettin' shot."

James put the cork back in the bottle tossed it to Thomas, who caught it in one hand. "That's why I got a bottle, and not a beer mug."

"Thanks." Thomas took a swig himself, and tossed it back.

"Okay," Thomas said, "time to find out what's goin' on."

"And how do you expect to do that?"

"The easy way," Thomas said. "Ask."

"I told you not to get excited!" Red yelled at Harry. "I told you not to fire until I did."

Red looked at Gareth, who pointed at Harry.

"Don't blame us," he said. "We only started firin' when he did."

"Was either one of them hit?" Red asked Gareth.

"Didn't look like it to me," the man answered, "but we've got them pinned down. Tutt's got the back covered."

"Okay."

Red walked to the front of the building they were in, which was right across the street from the cantina. Cutler and Shaw were at the windows with rifles. There were no people on the street. Word had gotten around that two *gringos* were going to come riding in, and there would be shooting. Tutt had been on the roof of one of the buildings, keeping watch. When he saw the two riders, he sounded the alarm, then took up his position behind the cantina.

Everything was in place for a successful ambush — until Harry got excited.

"I'm sorry, Red," Harry said. "I saw that deputy's back turned and —"

"I know, Harry." Red tapped his brother's cheek lightly, then suddenly slapped him. The sound was like a shot in the room. Harry staggered back, his hand to his face, while the others looked on.

"I oughtta send you out there!" Red said. "As bait!"

"Red! You shouldn't —"

"Shut up!"

Red turned to Gareth, who said, "Now what?"

"We could burn them out," Red said.

"You light that place on fire," Gareth said, "and that whole side of the street'll go up.

335

That happens, it won't be long before the whole town burns down."

Red scowled.

"You want that?" Gareth asked.

"I don't really care, but . . ."

"You like this place, don't ya?" Gareth asked.

Red shrugged. "It's a town, like any other town."

"It's where you lie low, though."

"Yeah, well, we kill them two Shaye brothers, I won't be lyin' low here much longer. And so far I've managed to steer clear of the *federales*. I burn this town down, that won't be the case."

"We kill them two lawmen here, the *federales* won't like that, either."

"Well," Red said, "we'll kill 'em and then get outta here, back to the States. Nobody'll be the wiser."

"The sheriff here won't tell 'em?"

"Not a word," Red said. "Not so long as I pay 'im."

"Or kill 'im."

"And then we're back to dealin' with the *federales*. Now, I think we'll —"

Red was cut off by a voice from across the street.

"Red! Red Fleming? You there?"

Red moved to the doorway, looked at the

336

cantina. Nobody was in sight, but that's where the voice was coming from.

"Red?"

"I hear ya, Deputy!" Red called back.

"I wanna talk."

"You're talkin'!"

"Meet me outside."

"Not a chance!" Red said. "Your brother will drill me."

"And your men will kill me. We'll both be at risk. Come on, let's talk."

Red hesitated.

"You gonna do it?" Gareth asked.

"Why not?" Red said. "Maybe I can get him to face me. Then we can kill the other one."

"How do you know which one is talkin'?" Gareth asked.

Red grinned. "I know."

"You can't go out there!" James said.

Thomas took off his gunbelt, handed it to his brother.

"I'm stallin' for time," Thomas said. "Meanwhile, maybe I can talk him out of this. This town's got to have a lawman. Maybe he'll show up."

"You think so?"

"No," Thomas said. "Down here, the law is probably takin' money from Red."

"What am I supposed to do?" James asked. "Watch you die?"

"If he or his men kill me, you kill him."

"And then I'm on my own," James said.

"And then you'll be on your own."

SIXTY-TWO

Thomas stepped out of the cantina. Moments later, Red Fleming stepped from the building across the street. Neither of them was wearing a gun. At that same moment, they stepped into the street and started walking. They met in the middle.

"I knew it would be you," Red said.

"How?"

"You're the older one," Red said, "like me. You're the gun hawk, like me. What's on your mind?"

"Stayin' alive."

"Funny," Red said, "that's what's on my mind. Seems like we have a lot in common. Like weaker little brothers."

"Only my brother's not weak," Thomas said. "If anybody puts a bullet in me, he'll kill you."

"Then he'll be dead."

"But so will you and me," Thomas said. "We won't know what's goin' on."

"So? You got a proposition?"

"I do," Thomas said. It had occurred to him just as he was crossing the street. "You and me, Red. Your brother says you're fast. Let's see how fast."

"And then what?"

"If I kill you, we all go free," Thomas said.

"And if I kill you?"

"Well, you could let my brother go, but somehow I don't believe you would."

"No, I wouldn't."

"Well," Thomas said, "first things first. You and me. What about it?"

"Why not?" Red asked. "Should be interestin'. You're supposed to be pretty fast."

"So are you. I don't suppose your men would go along with any decision you make if I end up killin' you."

"Probably not," Red said. "My brother might not let them."

"Well, we need to agree on one thing."

"What's that?"

"Whichever of us survives has to be allowed to get back across the street, and not be shot down."

"Sure, why not?" Red said. "I'd like the chance to get back to cover."

"What makes you think it'll be you?"

"I guess we'll find out," Red said. "That's what makes it interestin'."

They talked a little longer, then both turned and returned to their building. James watched nervously with his gun ready. If anything happened to his brother, Red Fleming wouldn't be able to take one more step.

When Thomas came back in, James released the breath he was holding.

"So?"

"He'll go for it."

"Go for what?"

"I got him to agree to a one-on-one between him and me."

"What's that accomplish?"

"I get to kill him."

"And if he kills you?"

"Then you get to kill him."

"That's your big plan?"

Thomas took his gunbelt from James and said, "Let me know if you think of a better one. You've got thirty seconds."

"This is crazy!" Harry said as Red took his gunbelt back.

"No it ain't," Red said, strapping it on. "I get to kill the deputy who arrested you."

"And then what?" Harry asked.

"And then we all get to kill the other one."

"And what are we supposed to do if he kills you?" Gareth asked.

341

"That'll be up to you and my brother," Red said. "Harry knows where I've got some money stashed. He'll be able to pay you all."

"If we kill the other brother," Gareth said.

"Right."

That brought back to Gareth's mind the idea of burning the deputy out. He didn't really care if the whole town went up in flames.

"But I'll be back," Red said.

"How sure are you?" Gareth asked,

"Dead sure."

"I wish I was as confident," the man said.

"My brother's the fastest gun alive!" Harry said. "If he says he'll be back, he'll be back."

Gareth pointed at Harry. "You just make sure you remember where that money is."

"Okay," Red said, adjusting his gunbelt. "I'm ready. This is gonna be a fair fight. Nobody shoots — unless he kills me. Got it?"

"We got it," Gareth said.

"Red —"

Red put his hand on his brother's shoulder and said, "I'll be right back."

"You better be."

Red smiled and stepped out the door.

■ ■ ■ ■

"No better ideas?" Thomas asked.

"Not in thirty seconds!"

"Then I'm doin' this."

"Are you gonna be able to outdraw him?"

"I won't know until I try, James."

James grabbed a handful of his brother's shirt front.

"Pa always says you're faster than he is!"

"That would be comfortin' if Pa's reputation was as a fast gun, but it's not. It's as a tough lawman."

"Just don't get killed!" James said.

"I'll do my best."

They both peered out the door.

"There he is," James said.

Thomas put his hand on his brother's shoulder and said, "I'll be right back."

"You better be!"

SIXTY-THREE

Thomas and Red Fleming stood in front of their respective doorways for a minute, then stepped down into the street. Instead of approaching each other, they began moving to their right, looking for an advantage. Because of the position of the sun and location of the town, neither would have the sun at their back.

But Thomas wanted James to have a clear shot at Red Fleming, and Red wanted his men to have a clear shot at Thomas Shaye. So they moved until they were both standing in the center of the street, with buildings on either side.

And facing each other . . .

"Are we gonna do this?" Harry asked. "Just watch?"

"That's what Red wants," Gareth said. "He's the boss."

"If he gets killed —"

"Just keep watchin', little brother," Gareth said, "and remember where that money is. Whether he comes back in here or not, we're gonna wanna get paid."

"You'll get paid," Harry said, "after both those deputies are dead."

Gareth looked at Harry. "Spoken like your brother."

James didn't have a rifle, and the shotgun was worthless for this. The buckshot pattern would be too wide by the time it reached Red Fleming to do more than sting him. So he put the shotgun down and drew his gun.

As he watched, the sweat came pouring down his brow, and it had nothing to do with the Mexican heat.

Thomas felt the sweat rolling down his back. His father had once told him if you weren't afraid during a gunfight, you weren't approaching it with the right mindset.

"There's always gonna be a faster gun than you out there, son," Dan Shaye said, "and one day he'll find you."

So Thomas had to wonder.

Was today the day?

Red Fleming had lost track of the number of men he'd killed. He didn't count. That wasn't what was important to him. What was important was that he walked away, every time, with not a scratch.

And that was what he expected to happen, this time.

Who made the first move didn't usually matter.

It was who made the last move that counted.

Thomas couldn't see Red's eyes, so he watched the man's shoulders, not his hands.

"You'll usually see a man's move in his shoulder, first," Dan Shaye had told him years ago. "Watch for it."

Thomas watched, and there was the slightest hitch in Red Fleming's shoulder just before he went for his gun.

"The fast draw ain't the thing," his father had also told him. "It's the shot that counts. It's got to be accurate."

Thomas drew and fired.

As Harry watched, Thomas's bullet struck Red in the chest before Red could draw his gun. He watched his older brother stagger back and fall to the ground, and then went for his own gun.

Gareth grabbed his wrist and stopped him.

"Red said a fair fight."

"You wanna get paid?" Harry demanded. "You kill that sonofabitch now or nobody gets paid. Understand?"

It didn't take Gareth a tenth of a second to make up his mind.

"Gun 'im!" he snapped to his men.

James was relieved when Red Fleming fell onto his back, but he didn't take the time to celebrate. Thomas was still out there in the middle of the street. He saw the rifle barrels across the street push out the window, and he started firing.

Thomas waited a full second too long.

Red Fleming was dead, and he was alive. It took him that full second to process the information, and then he was moving as the shots started.

There was a horse trough in front of the cantina, and he dove for it. At the same time, his and James's horses panicked, pulled free of the hitching post and ran off. For a moment the horses shielded Thomas from view. By the time the horses were gone, he was behind the trough and lead was slamming into it, puncturing it with holes from which the water poured out.

He got to his knees and, while James reloaded, he started to fire. They were still

347

outgunned, but at least something was happening now.

The waiting was over.

And then, suddenly, riders were coming down the street at full speed. He looked to see who it was, and saw the company of *federales* they had been hiding from for days.

The man in charge was at the head of the column, and he started barking orders. Before long, the uniformed *federales* were leading Harry Fleming and his men out into the street, and doing the same to Thomas and James.

Sheriff Pedro Arroyo came running up the street and started chattering in Spanish with the commander.

The *federales* put all the men together on one side of the street and covered them.

"I wonder what they're sayin'," James asked.

"The sheriff is telling the captain that he didn't know what was happenin' in his town until the shootin' started," Gareth translated. "The captain doesn't believe him."

"Good," Thomas said.

And then the *federales* took the sheriff's gun, ripped the badge from his shirt, and lined him up with the others.

The captain walked to the body of Red Fleming, looked at it for a moment, then came back.

"You," he said, pointing at Harry. "That was your brother?"

"Yeah," Harry said, "and those men killed him. Shot him down in cold blood."

"That's not true!" James snapped. "They were tryin' to kill us. We're lawmen from Arizona —"

"I know who you are, *señor,*" the captain said. "You will kindly be silent, please." He turned his attention back to Harry. "I warned you and your brother, *señor,* not to break the law in Mexico. Now you will pay the price."

"Me?" Harry shouted. "What about them?"

The captain turned to his sergeant and gave an order in rapid Spanish. Abruptly, Harry Fleming and the other men were herded together and marched away, with Harry still shouting. The sheriff was taken with them.

Then and only then did the captain turn his attention to Thomas and James.

"Those men will be going to a Mexican prison," he said.

"And us?" Thomas asked.

"You will be escorted to the border, where you will leave Mexico and not return."

"Agreed," Thomas said.

"Wait a minute!" James said. "We came here for Harry Fleming."

"Is he the brother of that one?" the captain asked, pointing to the body of Red Fleming.

"Yes," Thomas said. He looked at James. "We got Red, James. We can let the Mexicans have Harry."

"But we don't know which one of them killed —"

"You will mount up and ride," the captain ordered. "I will send several men to escort you. Ah, here are your horses."

Thomas and James turned and saw a uniformed *federale* leading their horses back.

"What, now?" James asked. "We're to leave right now?"

"How do you Americans say it?" the captain asked. "The sooner the better!"

Sixty-Four

Shaye looked Vin Packer up and down.

"Are you ready, Vin?" Doucette asked.

"I've been ready, Mr. Doucette," Vin said.

Doucette looked at Shaye.

"I don't suppose you'd want to take off that badge, drop it in the dirt, and walk away?"

"No," Shaye said.

"I didn't think so. You're not the type."

"What type am I, Doucette?"

"The type who'll die with that stupid silver star on your chest."

"And you," Shaye said. "You're the type to let other men do your killin' for you."

Doucette smiled.

"I know my limitations, Sheriff," Doucette said. "I can kill the mayor easily. You're another matter. For you I need a specialist."

"And you've robbed the cradle to get one," Shaye said.

"Hear that, Vin?" Doucette said. "The

351

sheriff's not taking you seriously."

"That would be a mistake, sir," Vin said. Shaye wasn't sure if he was talking to Doucette, or to him.

"All right, then," Shaye said, "let's get it over with."

"That's exactly how I feel," Doucette said.

Shaye moved into the street with the kid. It immediately became apparent something was going to happen. People started to gather; word had begun to get around.

"There you go, Vin," Doucette said. "You're gettin' your crowd."

"Whenever you're ready, Mr. Shaye," Vin said.

"That's okay, son," Shaye said, watching the boy's shoulders. "You make the first move."

"I'll outdraw you clean," Vin warned.

It's not the draw that counts . . .

The boy actually had a terrible hitch in his shoulder just before he was going to draw. Shaye wondered how he had survived this long. Then he saw why. Despite the hitch, Vin's draw was incredibly fast. He outdrew Shaye clean as a whistle, but by then Shaye was moving, throwing himself to the ground as he drew, and rolling. By the time he came to a stop, Vin had fired twice, sending his bullets to where Shaye had been standing. Shaye fired from the ground and drilled the boy right through the chest. Vin staggered back, a look of amazement on his young face, and then he crumpled rather than fell.

Shaye got to his feet quickly and looked at Doucette, who was still sitting in his chair, looking calm.

"Well," the outlaw said, "that was something to see. He outdrew you clean, Sheriff."

"Yes, he did."

Shaye walked to the boy's body, kicked the gun away, bent just to make sure he was dead. Then he holstered his gun, slapped the dirt of the street off the front of his clothes, and walked over to Doucette.

"Let me have your gun, Cole, and we'll take a walk to the jail."

"You're arresting me?"

"I am."

"For what? I never moved from this chair."

"We'll come up with somethin'," Shaye assured him.

Doucette's men were surprised to see him in the jail.

"You finally come to get us out?" Santini asked.

"Sorry, boys," Shaye said, "but Mr. Doucette is checkin' in."

Because he had so many of Doucette's men in cells, he'd had to double up. Now he had to add Doucette to a cell, making three people in that cell. Only the other two weren't real happy with Doucette for leaving them in there all this time.

"Well, well," Ledbetter said to Santini, "look who's joinin' the party. The big man himself."

"What happened to the kid?" Santini asked Shaye. "Packer?"

"He's dead."

"Ha!" Ledbetter said, looking at Doucette, "he was your secret weapon, right?"

Doucette smiled. "I've got other aces up my sleeve."

Shaye unlocked the door to the cell holding Ledbetter and Santini.

"You can't put me in there with them," Doucette said. "I want my own cell."

"Sorry. Can't oblige you," Shaye said. "We're full up."

"Then put them in with somebody else," Doucette said, getting agitated. "I want my own cell."

Shaye opened the door and said, "Get in there."

The two men were smiling in anticipation. First he made them leave the Renegade Saloon when they were having a good time, then they got arrested and he left them in these cells for days. Time for a little payback.

"Look, Shaye," Doucette said, "this isn't right —"

Shaye put his hand against Doucette's back and shoved him into the cell. Ledbetter and Santini caught him, each holding onto one arm.

"Take it up with them."

EPILOGUE

One week later . . .

When Thomas and James came riding back into Vengeance Creek it seemed quiet — too quiet. It was just after noon, and the streets should have been busy with people.

"I don't like the way this feels," James said. "Let's find Pa."

They rode directly to the sheriff's office, dismounted and went inside. To their relief, Dan Shaye was seated at his desk.

"Well, well, look who finally decided to come back," Shaye said, smiling at his two boys. "Where'd you go, all the way to Mexico?"

"Well," James said, "yeah."

"We had to, Pa," Thomas said. "That's where the Flemings were, and we couldn't let them get away."

"So you got 'em?" Shaye asked. "They're outside?"

"Not exactly," James said.

"Then what, exactly?"

"Red's dead," James said. "Thomas had to kill him in a fair fight."

"And?"

"Harry's in a Mexican prison, by now," Thomas said. "With the rest of the Fleming gang."

"How did that work out?"

Thomas and James sat and told the story, taking turns with aspects of it.

"So Candy's dead, Red's dead, Harry's locked away, and so are those other men who didn't have anythin' to do with what happened here."

"Right," James said.

"But they were tryin' to kill us."

"But Capitan Salazar stopped them."

"Pretty much," James said.

"Hey, wait a minute," Thomas said. "How'd you know about Capitan Salazar?"

Shaye grinned. "He sent me a telegram askin' if my two sons were dumb enough to ride into Mexico with no authority. I told him they sure were, and that I'd consider it a personal favor if he'd escort you boys to the border safely."

"So that's why we're not also in a Mexican prison," James said.

"Yep," Shaye said, "that's why."

"Well . . . thanks, Pa," Thomas said.

"You're welcome, boys, and welcome home."

"So what's been goin' on since we left?" Thomas asked. "Did Cole Doucette ever show up."

"Oh yeah," Shaye said, "he's in a cell, been there for the better part of a week."

"What?" Thomas said. He and James got up and took a look into the cell block. They saw a single man in a cell, who looked somewhat the worse for wear.

"What happened to him?" James asked

"He had a disagreement with some of his men he was sharing a cell with."

"A disagreement?"

"They beat his ass!" Shaye said.

He explained how he'd come to have most of Doucette's men in jail, and how Doucette had made no attempt to get them out. He told them about Doucette's secret weapon, Vin Packer.

"So where are the other men?" Thomas asked.

"Well, they didn't really do anythin'," Shaye said, "so I fined them and sent them on their way. They were all so mad at Doucette, they just rode out of town."

"But why is he still here?" Thomas asked. "Didn't you take him before Judge Fairly?"

"I was going to," Shaye said, "until the

judge turned up dead."

"What?" James asked.

"Somebody shot him on the street one night."

"Doucette's men?" Thomas asked.

"I don't think so," Shaye said. "Doucette claims he still has an ace up his sleeve, but I ain't seen it."

"So now you're waitin' for another judge?" James asked.

"Exactly."

"And how did Doucette react to that?"

"He's still a little sore," Shaye said, "but he's also too damn cocky for my taste. I'm sure he had the judge killed, and the mayor may be next."

"Or you," James said.

"Or me," Shaye agreed. "He may figure if he has all three of us taken care of, he'll go scot free."

"Well," Thomas said, "he'd have to take care of us, too."

"I'll make sure he knows that," Shaye said. "Meanwhile, why don't you boys go on home, get cleaned up and then come back, and I'll buy you the biggest damn steaks you ever saw."

"That sounds good to me," James said. "I've had enough beans and enchiladas to last me a lifetime."

Both boys stood up, left the office and headed back home to the house they shared with their father.

The three Shayes were in the Rawhide Steak House. Thomas and James enjoyed the steaks their father had promised them. They each told him a little more about what had happened, both before they'd met up and after.

"You got shot?" Shaye asked Thomas. "Why didn't you start off with that? You seen a doctor?"

"Yes," Thomas said. "I'm stitched up good and proper."

"Well, maybe you should see Doc Stone anyway."

"Tomorrow," Thomas said.

"So people are stayin' off the street since the judge got killed?" James asked.

"That's right," Shaye said. "Nobody wants to get shot."

"And what's this ace Doucette keeps talkin' about?" James asked.

"I think if we find the ace, we find the killer," Shaye said.

At that moment the door to the restaurant opened and a well-dressed man stepped in.

"Speakin' of killers . . ." Shaye said.

"Who's that, Pa?" James asked.

"That's Tate Kingdom."

"Kingdom?" Thomas asked. "When did he get to town?"

"He's been here a while. Actually backed a play or two of mine. I thought he'd leave town after I locked up Doucette, but he hasn't. He spends his days playing low-stakes poker in the Renegade."

"You mean he ain't killed anybody?" James asked.

Before Shaye could answer, Kingdom walked over to their table.

"These must be your sons," he said.

"That's right, Kingdom. They got back a little while ago."

"That's good," Kingdom said. "You got your deputies back. You won't be needing me anymore."

"No, he won't," James said.

"But we appreciate the help you gave him while we were gone," Thomas added.

"You boys mind if I join you?" Kingdom asked, then sat before anyone answered.

"What's on your mind, Kingdom?" Shaye asked. "Why are you still in town?"

"Well, to tell you the truth, Sheriff," Kingdom said, "I've still got a little job to do."

"A job?"

"That's right."

"I thought you were just passin' through?"

"Well, that was a little lie."

"Really?" Shaye asked. "Anythin' else you might have lied about?"

Kingdom reached into his pocket and tossed something into the center of the table. The Shayes saw that it was an Ace of Spades.

"What's that supposed to mean?" James asked.

"It's the ace, James," Thomas said.

"Huh?"

"So you're Doucette's ace," Shaye said.

"That's right."

"Been workin' for him the whole time?"

"The whole time."

"And Vin Packer wasn't his surprise."

"That boy?" Kingdom said. "I knew you'd kill him, Dan."

"So why did you wait so long to come forward?"

"Actually," Kingdom said, "I'm moving up my timetable because your boys got back."

"You killed the judge," Shaye said, "then you were gonna kill the mayor, and then me."

"Well," Kingdom said, "I'm not going to admit to killing the judge. That'd be stupid. You'd arrest me."

362

"What makes you think I won't arrest you, anyway?"

"I haven't done anything — anything you can prove, that is. And you don't have your judge to back any trumped-up charges."

"So what's next?" Shaye asked.

"You and me, Dan," Kingdom said, "out on the street."

"You know," Shaye said, "I could arrest you right here and now."

Kingdom shook his head. "That'd get messy. Too many people in here, even though it's not fully supper time. Out on the street it'll just be you and me."

"You'll kill me easy," Shaye said.

"Probably."

"It'd be stupid of me to agree."

"You don't have a choice," Kingdom said.

"Yes," Thomas said, "he does."

Kingdom looked at Thomas. "You?"

"Me."

"Stand up for your father, huh?"

"My father, the badge, the town . . . take your pick."

"You know that after I kill you, I'd kill him, anyway."

"And you'd have to kill me," James said.

Kingdom looked at James. "That would make me sad."

"But first," Shaye said, "you have to get

363

past Thomas."

"So you'd have your son fight your battle for you?"

"You know," Shaye said, "a man just told me recently that you've got to know your limitations."

"I guess he was right," Kingdom said. He looked at Thomas. "Let's walk out together, son. I don't want to step outside and then have the three of you come out after me."

"Suits me," Thomas said. He looked at his father. "Order me dessert. Apple pie."

Shaye nodded, watched Kingdom and Thomas walk out the door together. The people at the other tables quickly got up and ran to the windows.

"Pa —"

"Stay where you are, James."

"But Pa —"

"We've got to order Thomas his pie. You want any?"

"Pa, what if he don't —"

"I'm havin' peach."

He waved a waiter over. The man reluctantly detached himself from a window.

"Two pieces of apple pie, and one peach."

"Uh, yessir. Right away."

As the waiter walked back to the kitchen there were two shots from outside. He hunched his shoulders and kept going.

"Pa —" James said.

He was interrupted when the door opened and Thomas walked in.

"Pa," James said, "I'd rather have rhubarb."

"You and your mother," Shaye said, shaking his head, "never understood how you could eat that."

ABOUT THE AUTHOR

The first 3 Sons of Daniel Shaye books — *Leaving Epitaph, Vengeance Creek* and *Pearl River Junction* — were published in 2004, 2005 and 2006.

Robert J. Randisi is the creator and author of the long running Gunsmith Western series as "J. R. Roberts," as well as the upcoming series, Lady Gunsmith.

He is the author of the "Miles Jacoby," "Nick Delvecchio," "Gil & Claire Hunt," "Dennis McQueen," "Joe Keough," and "The Rat Pack" mystery series. *The Honky Tonk Big Hoss Boogie* (Perfect Crime Books), the first book in the Auggie Velez Nashville P.I. series, appeared in 2013. The second book, *The Last Sweet Song of Hammer Dylan,* appeared in 2017.

His recent novel, *Mckenna's House*, has been called his best book yet by several reviewers. His "Housesitting Detective" series appeared in 2015, with the first book, *Dry Stone Walls.*

The 10th book in his Rat Pack series, *When Somebody Kills You,* was published in 2015. The 11th book, *I Only Have Lies for You,* published in 2017.

He is the editor of over 30 anthologies. All told he has had more than 650 books published.

He is the founder of the Private Eye Writers of America, and the creator of the Shamus Award. He is also the co-founder of Mystery Scene Magazine and the American Crime Writers League with Ed Gorman, and one of the founders of Western Fictioneers and the Peacemaker Award. In addition, he was the editor of PWA's *How to Write a P.I. Novel* for Writer's Digest.